'Following the enormous success of Lauren's stunning interpretation of Pippi Longstocking in 2007, we were delighted when Lauren agreed to create a new edition of Pippi Goes Aboard. Lauren is the perfect illustrator to interpret my grandmother's work: she understands Pippi's psyche and motivation, shares her playfulness, sense of generosity and adventure. Her quirky illustrations pop off the page embodying the fun and mischief Pippi is so well known and loved for. Lauren, like the character she has enjoyed a life-long passion for, is an artist unafraid to subvert convention. Who better to bring Pippi alive for a new generation of free spirits! We hope you enjoy this beautiful edition as much as we at the Astrid Lindgren Company have.'

Olle Nyman, grandson of Astrid Lindgren and CEO of The Astrid Lindgren Company

For Jo L.C.

OXFORD
UNIVERSITY PRESS

Great Clarendon Street, Oxford OX2 6DP

Oxford University Press is a department of the University of Oxford.
It furthers the University's objective of excellence in research, scholarship,
and education by publishing worldwide. Oxford is a registered trade mark
of Oxford University Press in the UK and in certain other countries

© Text: Astrid Lindgren 1946 The Astrid Lindgren Company
© Illustrations: Lauren Child 2020

Translated by Susan Beard, used by agreement with The Astrid Lindgren Company.

First published in 1946 by Rabén & Sjögren, Sweden as *Pippi Långstrump Går Ombord*

For more information about Astrid Lindgren, see www.astridlindgren.com.
All foreign rights are handled by The Astrid Lindgren Company, Lidingö, Sweden.
For more information, please contact info@astridlindgren.se.

The moral rights of the author have been asserted

Database right Oxford University Press (maker)

First published 1946
This edition 2020

All rights reserved. No part of this publication may be reproduced,
stored in a retrieval system, or transmitted, in any form or by any means,
without the prior permission in writing of Oxford University Press,
or as expressly permitted by law, or under terms agreed with the appropriate
reprographics rights organization. Enquiries concerning reproduction
outside the scope of the above should be sent to the Rights Department,
Oxford University Press, at the address above

You must not circulate this book in any other binding or cover
and you must impose this same condition on any acquirer

British Library Cataloguing in Publication Data

Data available

ISBN: 978-0-19-277507-8

1 3 5 7 9 10 8 6 4 2

Printed in China

Paper used in the production of this book is a natural,
recyclable product made from wood grown in sustainable forests.
The manufacturing process conforms to the environmental
regulations of the country of origin.

Designed by David Mackintosh

Astrid Lindgren

Pippi Longstocking
GOES ABOARD

Illustrated by Lauren Child

Translated by Susan Beard

OXFORD
UNIVERSITY PRESS

CONTENTS

CHAPTER ONE
Pippi Still Lives in Villa Villekulla
6

CHAPTER TWO
Pippi Goes Shopping
16

CHAPTER THREE
Pippi Writes a Letter and Goes to School—But Not for Long
46

CHAPTER FOUR
Pippi Goes on the School Outing
62

CHAPTER FIVE
Pippi and Market Day
82

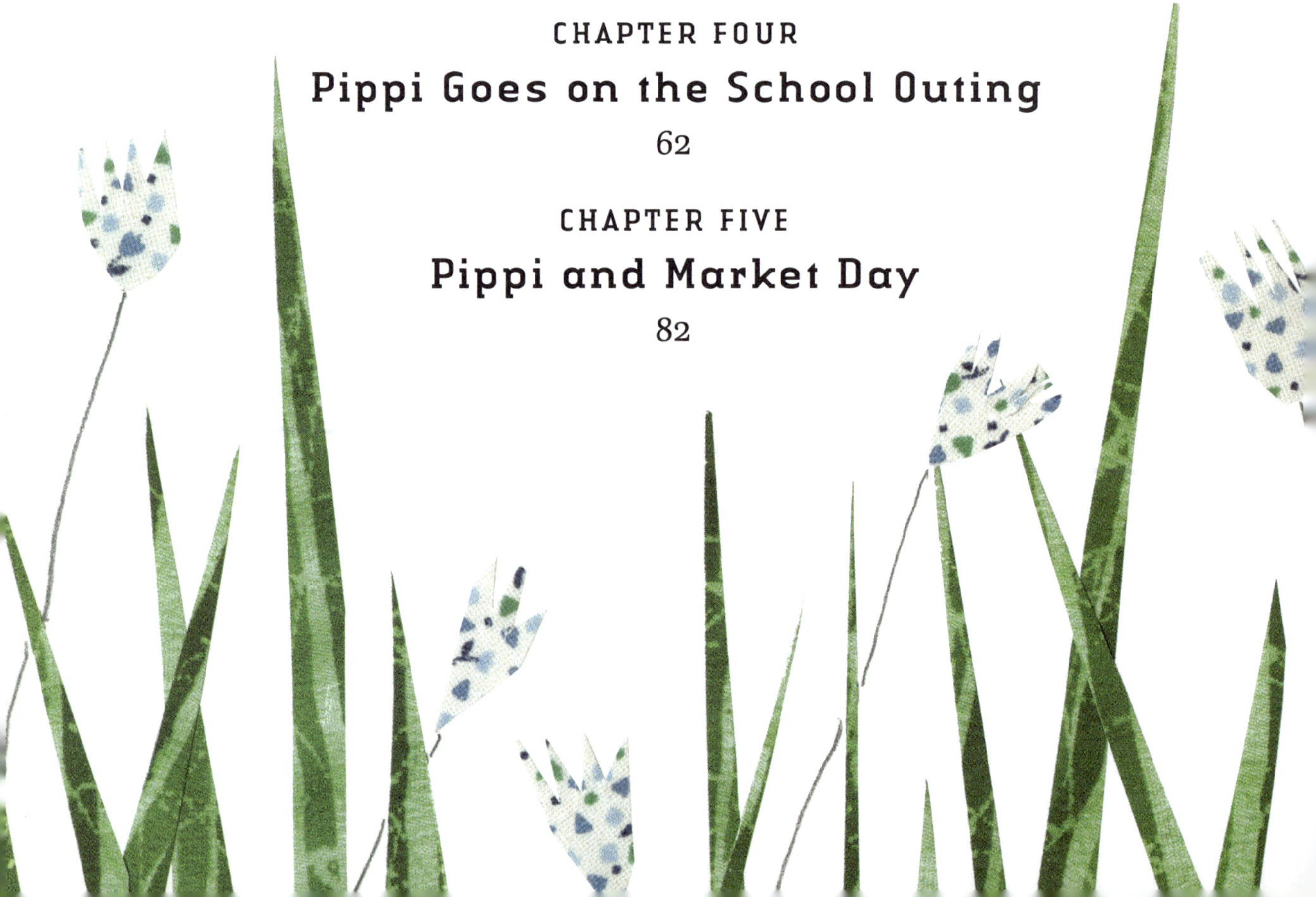

CHAPTER SIX
Pippi is Shipwrecked
110

CHAPTER SEVEN
Pippi Has a Special Visitor
144

CHAPTER EIGHT
Pippi Has a Leaving Party
164

CHAPTER NINE
Pippi Goes Aboard
186

ABOUT THE AUTHOR
AND ILLUSTRATOR 206

Pippi Still Lives in Villa Villekulla

Chapter One

If a stranger should happen to travel to the tiny little town and perhaps quite by accident find he has wandered too far in one direction, he would see Villa Villekulla. Not that the house was much to look at, being quite an old and run-down sort of house, sitting in quite an old and overgrown garden, but the stranger might stop anyway and wonder who owned it. Naturally, all the people living in the tiny little town knew who lived in Villa Villekulla, and they also knew why there was a horse on the veranda. But someone coming from anywhere else wouldn't know that, of course. So he would probably wonder. Especially if it was getting very late and was practically dark, and he caught sight of a little girl striding around the garden even though it was so late, not looking at all as if she was thinking of going to bed. He would be bound to think:

'I wonder why that little girl's mother hasn't told her it's bedtime? Every other child is in bed by now, that's for sure.'

For how would the visitor know that the little girl didn't have a mother? She didn't have a father either, for that matter, at least not one who was at home. Quite simply, she lived there all alone in Villa Villekulla. Well, perhaps not really all alone, to be absolutely accurate, because her horse lived on the veranda. And she had a monkey, too, called Mr Nilsson. But naturally, anyone visiting the town wouldn't know anything about that. If the little girl walked to the front gate—and it was very probable she would, because she liked chatting to people—he'd have the chance of getting a proper look at her. And no doubt he couldn't help thinking:

'That is the freckliest, most red-haired child I have ever seen.'

And then he might think:

'Actually, it's really nice to be freckly and red-haired. At least if you look as if you're bursting with life the way this child does.'

He might be interested to know the name of the freckly, red-haired girl skipping around in the twilight, and if he happened to be standing beside the gate all he had to do was ask:

'What's your name?'

And the answer, in a very bright and chirpy voice, was likely to be:

'My name is **Pippilotta** Victoriaria Tea-cosy Appleminta Ephraim's-daughter Longstocking, daughter of Captain Ephraim Longstocking, former terror of the high seas and now a South Sea Island king. But I'm called **Pippi** for short.'

Yes, that's right! The girl was none other than Pippi Longstocking, and if she said her dad was a South Sea Island king then that's what she believed. For her dad had once blown overboard and disappeared when he and Pippi were sailing the oceans, and because Pippi's dad was rather fat she was positively convinced he hadn't drowned. Very likely he had floated ashore on an island and become king of all the Koratutt people. And that's precisely what Pippi thought.

It might happen that the visitor had plenty of time and wasn't in any hurry to catch a train that evening, in which case he would stop and chat with Pippi for a while and eventually realize that she did live in Villa Villekulla all alone, apart from a horse and a monkey. And if the visitor was kind-hearted, he probably couldn't help thinking:

'What does the poor child *live* on, exactly?'

But he most definitely shouldn't trouble himself about that.

'I'm as rich as a mountain troll,' Pippi always said. And she was. She had a whole travelling bag full of golden coins her dad had given her. So the visitor needn't think Pippi went without anything. She managed extremely well, despite not having a mum or a dad. Except, of course, there was no one to tell her when it was bedtime. But Pippi had found a good way: she told herself! Sometimes she didn't tell herself until it was ten o'clock at night, because Pippi had never believed in the notion that children had to go to bed at seven. After all, that was when you were having most fun. So the visitor shouldn't be at all surprised to see Pippi striding around her garden, even though the sun had gone down and it was starting to feel a little chilly and Tommy and Annika had been snoring in their beds for ages. Who were Tommy and Annika? Oh, the visitor couldn't know that, either! Tommy and Annika were Pippi's friends, you see! They lived in the house next door to Villa Villekulla. It was a pity the visitor hadn't arrived a little earlier, because then he would have been able to see Tommy and Annika. He would have seen two very sweet, well-behaved children, that's for sure. Without a doubt he would have found Tommy and Annika at Pippi's if only he had turned up a little earlier, because Tommy and Annika ran over to Pippi's house every single day and were always with her, except when they were sleeping and when they were eating and when they were at school. But at this time of night they were fast asleep in their beds, of course, because Tommy and Annika had a mum and a dad, and both their mum and dad were convinced that it was best for children to go to bed at seven o'clock.

If the visitor to the town had a great deal of time to spare he might stay behind after Pippi said goodnight and walked off up her garden path, simply to see what she would get up to all on her own and whether she really *wasn't* going to go indoors to bed soon. He could stand behind the gatepost and peep round it cautiously. Then what if Pippi did what she sometimes did in the evening when she was in the mood for a little ride on her horse! What if she stepped onto the veranda, lifted the horse high into the air on her strong arms and carried him into the garden! That would make the visitor rub his eyes all right and wonder if he was dreaming!

'Oh, my goodness, what kind of child is this?' he might say, behind the gatepost. 'I do believe she can lift that horse up! This is the most remarkable child I have ever seen!'

And he was right. Pippi was the most remarkable child ever—in that town, at least. There might be more remarkable children in other places, but in the tiny little town there was no one quite like Pippi Longstocking. And nowhere, not in the little town or in any spot in the whole wide world, was there a child as strong as she was.

One beautiful spring day, when the sun was shining and the birds were chirruping and the ditches were flowing with water, Tommy and Annika skipped over to Pippi's house. Tommy had a couple of sugar cubes with him for Pippi's horse and he and Annika stayed for a minute or two on the veranda, patting the horse, before they carried on in to see Pippi. Pippi was fast asleep in her bed when they came in. She had her feet on the pillow and her head tucked underneath the covers. She always slept like that. Annika pinched her big toe and said:

'Wakey wakey!'

Mr Nilsson, the little monkey, was awake already and sitting on the lamp in the ceiling. Eventually something moved under the covers and all of a sudden a red head popped out. Pippi opened her bright eyes and smiled broadly.

'Ahoy there, is it you pinching my toes! I dreamed it was my dad checking to see if I had any corns.'

She sat on the edge of her bed and pulled on her stockings, one brown and the other black.

'You won't get corns, believe me, not as long as

you have these,' she said, pushing each foot into her long, black shoes that were exactly twice as long as her feet.

'Pippi,' said Tommy. 'What shall we do today? We've got a day off school, Annika and me!'

'Well, let's see,' Pippi said. 'We can't dance around the Christmas tree because we slung that out three months ago. Digging for gold would be quite fun, but that won't do either because we don't know where to look for it. Most of the gold is in Alaska, by the way, and you can't move for all the gold diggers there. No, we'll have to think up something else.'

'Yes, something that's fun,' said Annika.

Pippi braided her hair into two tight plaits that stuck straight out. She thought for a while.

'What about walking into town and doing some **shopping**,' she said.

'But we haven't got any money,' said Tommy.

'I have,' said Pippi. And to prove it she went straight away and opened her travelling bag that was crammed full of golden coins. She took an enormous fistful and shoved the coins into the front pocket on her apron.

'Now all I need is my hat and I'm ready to go,' she said. The hat was nowhere to be seen. Pippi looked first in the log box, but oddly enough it wasn't there. Then she looked inside the bread bin in the larder, but all it contained was a hairband, an alarm clock and a little dried up crust. She even looked on the hat rack but there was nothing there except a frying pan, a screwdriver and a piece of cheese.

'There's no order in nothing, and I can't find everything,' Pippi grumbled. 'But I've been looking for that piece of cheese for a long time, so it was lucky it turned up. Listen, hat!' she called out. 'Are you coming to the shops or not? If you don't come out immediately it'll be too late!'

No hat appeared.

'Well, he's got only himself to blame when he's being such an idiot. But I don't want to hear any moaning when I get home,' she said, sternly.

Shortly afterwards Tommy, Annika, and Pippi, with Mr Nilsson on her shoulder, could be seen trooping along the road towards town. The sun was shining very warmly, the sky was very blue, and the children were very happy. A trickling sound came from the ditch beside the road. It was a deep ditch with a lot of water in it.

'I like ditches,' Pippi said, and without a second thought she stepped down into the water. It came up over her knees, and when she really hopped about it splashed all over Tommy and Annika.

'I'm pretending to be a boat,' she said, and ploughed on through the water. But just as she spoke she tripped and disappeared under the surface.

'Or rather, a submarine,' she carried on, as if nothing had happened, when her nose came up again.

'Oh, Pippi, you're all wet,' Annika said, anxiously.

'And what's wrong with that?' said Pippi. 'Who said children have to be dry? We can all benefit from a cold wash, so I've heard. It's only here in this country that people think children shouldn't walk in ditches. In America the ditches are stuffed so full of kids there's no room for the water. They stay there all year round. In the winter they get frozen in, of course, with their heads poking out of the ice. Their mums have to go and give them blueberry soup and meatballs because they can't come home for dinner. But they are as fit as fleas, I can tell you that much!'

The little town looked very neat and tidy in the spring sunshine. The narrow, cobbled streets wound their way higgledy-piggledy between the buildings. Snowdrops and crocuses were springing up in the small flower beds surrounding most of the houses. There were plenty of shops in the little town and on this lovely spring day there were a lot of people going in and out, and the shop door bells were ringing nonstop. Housewives came along with baskets over their arms to buy coffee and sugar and soap and butter. A few of the town's children were also out, buying a lollipop or some bubblegum. But most children didn't have the money to buy anything, and they could only stand outside the shops and simply *look* at all the treats behind the panes of glass, poor things.

Just as the sun was shining at its best, three small figures appeared on Storgatan. They were Tommy, Annika, and a very soggy Pippi, who left a wet trail behind her as she strolled along.

'How lucky we are,' said Annika. 'Look, so many shops, and we've got a whole apron pocket full of golden coins.'

That made Tommy very happy, too, when he thought about it, and he skipped high into the air.

'Well, let's get started,' said Pippi. 'First of all, I'd like to **buy a piano**.'

'But Pippi,' Tommy said. 'You can't play the piano, can you?'

'How can I know that, when I've never tried?' said Pippi. 'I've never had a piano to try on. And let me tell you, Tommy, playing the piano without a piano takes a lot of practice.'

There didn't seem to be a piano shop. Instead, the

children walked past a shop that sold cosmetics. In the shop window was a large pot of cream, and beside the pot was a sign that said: **DO YOU SUFFER FROM FRECKLES?**

'What does that sign say?' asked Pippi.

She couldn't read all that well because she wouldn't go to school like other children.

'It says: "Do you suffer from freckles?"' said Annika.

'Does it indeed?' said Pippi, deep in thought. 'Well, a polite question deserves a polite answer. Come on, let's go in!'

She pushed open the door and stepped inside, closely followed by Tommy and Annika. A lady was standing behind the counter. Pippi walked straight up to her.

'**NO**,' she said, firmly.

'What can I do for you?' asked the lady.

'**NO**,' Pippi said again.

'I don't understand what you mean,' the lady said.

'**NO**, I *don't* suffer from freckles,' said Pippi.

Then the lady understood. And she took a close look at Pippi and burst out:

'But, you poor child, your entire face is covered in freckles!'

'Yes, it is,' said Pippi. 'But I don't suffer from them. I like them! Good morning!'

And out she went again. In the doorway she turned round and shouted:

'But if you get any cream that gives you even *more* freckles, you can send me about seven or eight pots.'

Next door was a shop selling ladies' clothes.

'We haven't done very well with our shopping so far,' said Pippi. 'We'd better try harder.'

They trooped in, first Pippi, then Tommy and then Annika. The first thing they saw was a very fine shop dummy dressed in a blue silk dress. Pippi walked over to the dummy and took her hand in a warm greeting.

'Morning, morning,' Pippi said. 'You are the lady who runs the shop, I believe? How terribly nice to meet you,' and she shook the dummy's hand even more warmly.

But then a dreadful accident happened:

the dummy's arm came loose 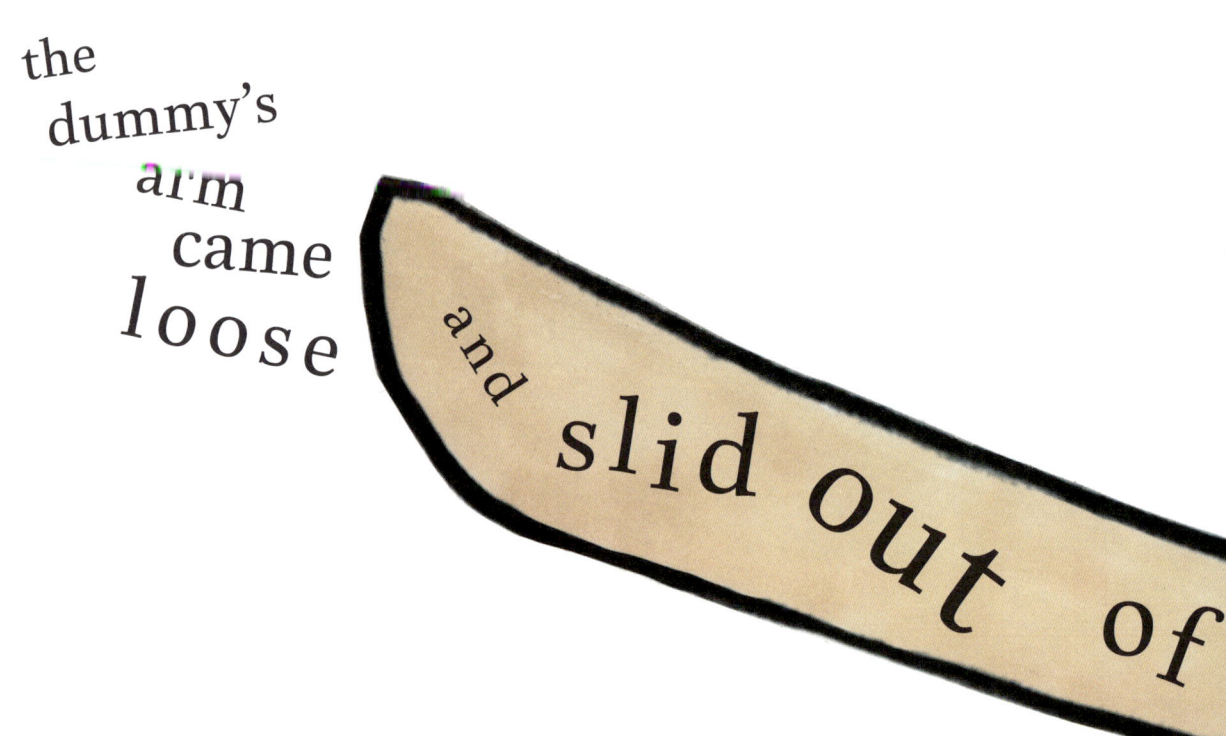 and slid out of

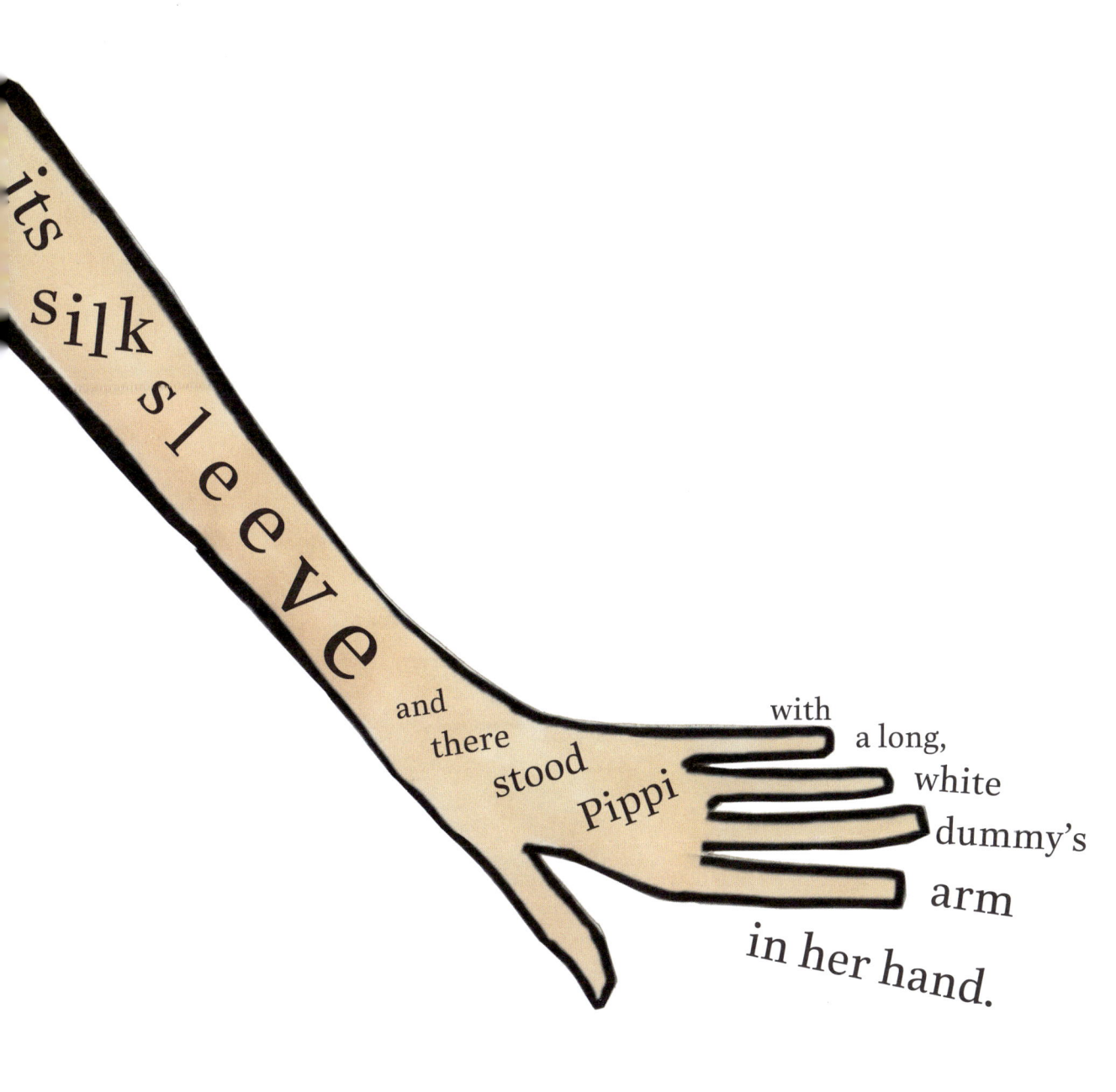

its silk sleeve and there stood Pippi with a long, white dummy's arm in her hand.

Tommy gasped in horror and Annika almost cried. The shop assistant came running up and began giving Pippi a good telling off.

'Calm down a kilo or three,' said Pippi, when she had listened for a while. 'I thought it was self-service here, and I was planning to buy this arm.'

That made the shop assistant even angrier and she said the dummy wasn't for sale. And anyway, she couldn't sell only one arm. Pippi was jolly well going to have to pay, whatever the whole dummy cost, seeing as she had damaged it.

'Extremely odd,' said Pippi. 'It's lucky they're not this **daft** in every shop. What if I wanted to eat mashed swede and pork, and I went to the butcher to buy the pork and he tried to make me take the whole pig?'

While she was talking she fished some golden coins out of her apron pocket and slapped them down onto the counter. The shop assistant was stunned into silence.

'Does the old girl cost more than this?' Pippi asked.

'No, certainly not. Not nearly so much,' said the assistant, and bowed politely.

'Keep what's left over and buy something nice for

the children,' said Pippi, walking towards the door. The assistant ran behind her, bowing and bowing, and asked where she could send the shop window dummy.

'**All I want is this arm**, and I can take that with me,' said Pippi. 'You can share the rest out among the poor. Cheerio!'

'But what are you going to *do* with that arm?' asked Tommy, when they were out in the street again.

'This?' said Pippi. 'What do I want this for? Don't people have false hair and false teeth? And false noses sometimes? So why can't I have a little false arm? And by the way, let me tell you, it's very practical having three arms. I remember when Dad and I were sailing around on the ocean once and we came to a town where all the people had three arms. Handy, eh? Just imagine when they were eating and had a fork in one hand, a knife in the other and suddenly they had to pick their nose or scratch their ear, how easy it was to bring out a third arm. They saved a lot of time that way, I can tell you.'

Pippi looked thoughtful.

'Darn it, now I'm lying again,' she said. 'It's odd.

Suddenly all that lying bubbles up inside me and I can't do a thing about it. To be honest, they didn't have three arms at all in that town. They only had two.'

She fell silent for a moment, considering.

'A whole load of them only had one, actually,' she said. 'Yes, truth be told, there were even people who had none, and if they wanted to eat they had to lie down on the plate and slurp up their food. They couldn't scratch their ears at all, they had to ask their mum. That's how it was.'

Pippi shook her head sadly.

'The fact is, I've never seen so few arms anywhere else apart from that town. But that's just like me. I always have to make myself seem important and pretend people have more arms than they really do.'

Pippi marched on with the false arm thrown casually over one shoulder. Outside a sweet shop she came to a halt. There was a long line of children gazing longingly at all the delicious things arranged in the window. Big jars full of red and blue and green sweets, long rows of chocolate bars, stacks of bubblegum and the most tempting lollipops—yes, it wasn't surprising that the little children were standing there, sighing from time to time. Because they didn't have any money. Not even the tiniest five-öre piece.

'Pippi, shall we go in *this* shop?' Tommy asked eagerly, tugging at Pippi's dress.

'This is a shop we *will* go into,' said Pippi, decisively. 'A long way in!'

And they did.

'Please may I have **eighteen** kilos of sweets,' Pippi said, waving a golden coin. The shop assistant could only gape. She wasn't used to anyone buying so many sweets at one time.

'You mean you want eighteen sweets,' she said.

'I mean I want **eighteen** *kilos* of sweets,' said Pippi. She put the golden coin on the counter. Then the assistant hurried to shovel sweets into large bags. Tommy and Annika stood behind her and pointed out the best sweets. There were some really scrumptious red ones. After you had sucked on one of those for a while a lovely gooey mess suddenly filled your mouth. Then there were some green sour ones that weren't too bad, either. And jelly raspberries and liquorice boats were good, too.

'Let's take three kilos of each,' suggested Annika. And they did.

'And if I could now have **sixty** lollipops and **seventy-two** packets of toffees, I don't think I need anything else today, apart from a **hundred and three** chocolate cigarettes,' said Pippi. 'Unless you count a little trolley to carry it all in.'

The assistant said she thought they could buy a little trolley in the toyshop next door.

Outside the sweet shop there was now a large gathering of children, staring in through the window and practically fainting with excitement when they saw Pippi doing her shopping. Pippi charged into the toyshop, bought a pull-along trolley and loaded all her bags into it. She looked around, and then she called out: 'If there are any children here who don't eat sweets, please step forward!'

No one did.

'Highly unusual,' said Pippi. 'Well, are there any children here who *do* eat sweets?'

Twenty-three stepped forward. Including Tommy and Annika, naturally.

'Tommy, open the bags,' said Pippi.

So Tommy did.

And then such a sweet-eating began, never before seen in the little town.

All the children crammed their mouths full of sweets—the red ones with the gooey middles, the green sour ones, the liquorice boats, and the jelly raspberries, one after the other. And it was good to have a chocolate cigarette in your mouth at the same time, because the taste of the chocolate and the jelly raspberries was so good together. More children came running from every direction and Pippi gave out sweets by the handful.

'I think I'm going to have to buy another eighteen kilos,' she said. 'Otherwise there won't be any left for tomorrow.'

Pippi bought another eighteen kilos, but even then there weren't many left for tomorrow.

'Let's go to the next shop now,' said Pippi, and strode into the toyshop. All the children followed her. There were lots of nice things in the toyshop: trains and cars you could wind up, sweet little dolls in pretty dresses, dolls' tea sets, cap guns and tin soldiers, cuddly elephants and dogs, bookmarks and jumping jacks.

'What would you like?' asked the assistant.

'I'd like some of everything,' answered Pippi, running her eye over the shelves. 'We're **desperately**

short of jumping jacks, for example,' she went on. 'And cap guns. But I hope we can put that right.'

Then Pippi pulled out a handful of golden coins and the children could point to the things they thought they needed most. Annika settled on a wonderful doll with curly blonde hair and a pink satin dress. It could say 'Mamma' when its tummy was pressed. Tommy wanted an air rifle and a steam engine. And that's what he got. All the other children picked out what they wanted, and when Pippi had finished her shopping there wasn't an awful lot left on the shelves, apart from a few bookmarks and building bricks. Pippi didn't buy a single thing for herself, but Mr Nilsson got a little mirror.

Just before they left, Pippi bought every child a clay pipe in the shape of a cuckoo, and when the children came out onto the street they played their clay cuckoo pipes and Pippi directed them with the false arm.

One little boy complained that his pipe wasn't working. Pippi took it and had a look.

'Well, it's hardly surprising when there's bubblegum blocking the hole! Where did you get that little clump from? I didn't buy any bubblegum, as far as I know.'

'I've had it since Friday,' said the boy.

'And you're not worried about your jaws sticking together? Because that's how I thought **bubblegum-chewers** usually met their end.'

She handed the pipe back to the boy and he blew happily like all the others.

There was such a commotion on Storgatan that finally a policeman came to see what was going on.

'What's all this racket?' he shouted.

'It's the Kronoberg Regimental March,' Pippi said. 'But I'm not sure all the children know it that well. It seems some of them are playing "Make a Noise Like Thunder, Brothers".'

'Stop it this minute!' roared the policeman and clapped his hands over his ears. Pippi patted him on the back with the false arm, to comfort him.

'You should be glad we didn't buy trombones,' she said.

Gradually the cuckoo pipes fell silent, one by one. Eventually only Tommy's pipe was giving the occasional little squeak. The policeman told them very sternly that public gatherings were not allowed on Storgatan and the children must all go home. None of the children really minded. They were keen to play with their toy trains and drive their cars and make comfy beds for their dolls. So they all left together to go home, happy and content. They didn't eat any supper at all that day.

Pippi and Tommy and Annika were also going home. Pippi pulled the trolley behind her. She looked at all the shop signs they passed and tried to read them as best she could.

'**P-H-A-R-M-A-C-Y**. Oh, isn't that where you buy **meducine**?' she asked.

'Yes, that's where you buy *medicine*,' replied Annika.

'Well, in that case I must go in straight away and buy some,' said Pippi.

'But you're not ill,' Tommy said.

'If I'm not now, I might be later,' said Pippi. 'Every year masses of people get ill and die simply because they don't buy the right **meducine** in time. And it's out of the question anything like that will happen to me.'

Inside the pharmacy the pharmacist was pouring tablets into pots. But he wouldn't be pouring many more because it was getting late and would soon be time to close. Pippi, Tommy and Annika stepped up to the counter.

'Please may I have four litres of **meducine**,' said Pippi.

'What kind of medicine?' asked the pharmacist impatiently.

'Preferably the kind that's good for illnesses,' said Pippi.

'What kind of illnesses?' asked the pharmacist, getting even more impatient.

'Um, give me one that helps chicken pox and blisters and tummy ache and measles and a pea stuck up your nose, and things like that. It would be good if you could use it to polish furniture, too. A really powerful **meducine**.'

The pharmacist said there wasn't any medicine quite as powerful as that. You had to have different medicines for different ailments, he said, and when Pippi listed about ten other sicknesses she also wanted cured, he lined up a row of bottles on the counter. On some he wrote: "EXTERNAL USE" which meant the medicine could only be rubbed onto your skin. Pippi paid, took the bottles and left the shop.

Tommy and Annika followed her. The pharmacist looked at the clock and realized it was time to close. He locked the door after the children and looked forward to going home and having a bite to eat.

Outside the shop Pippi put the bottles down.

'Oh heck, I nearly forgot the most important thing,' she said.

Because the door was locked she put her finger on the bell and pressed hard for a long time. Tommy and Annika heard the bell jingling inside the shop. After a moment a little hatch in the door was opened—it was the hatch you could buy medicine from if you happened to fall ill during the night. The pharmacist poked out his head. He was rather red in the face.

'What do you want now?' he asked Pippi angrily.

'Excuse me, nice **Mr Pharmycist**,' Pippi said. 'But I just thought of something. Dear **Mr Pharmycist**, you know all about illnesses. What's the best thing to do when you've got a tummy ache—eating hot potato dumplings or soaking your tummy in cold water all night?'

The pharmacist's face went even redder.

'Hop it!' he shouted. 'Immediately! Otherwise . . . !'

He slammed the hatch shut.

She rang the bell once more and it wasn't many seconds before the pharmacist's face appeared in the hatch again. He really was tremendously red in the face.

'Hot potato dumplings might be a bit hard to digest,' Pippi suggested, peering up at him with her friendly eyes. The pharmacist didn't say anything. All he did was shut the hatch with a bang.

'Suit yourself,' said Pippi, shrugging her shoulders. 'Perhaps I'll try a hot potato dumpling anyway. He can blame himself if something goes horribly wrong.'

She sat down calmly on the step outside the pharmacy and lined up all her bottles.

'Grown-ups can be so impractical,' she said. 'Here I have, let me see, eight bottles, and it could all very easily fit into one. Lucky I've got a bit of common sense, I say.'

And   with   those   words

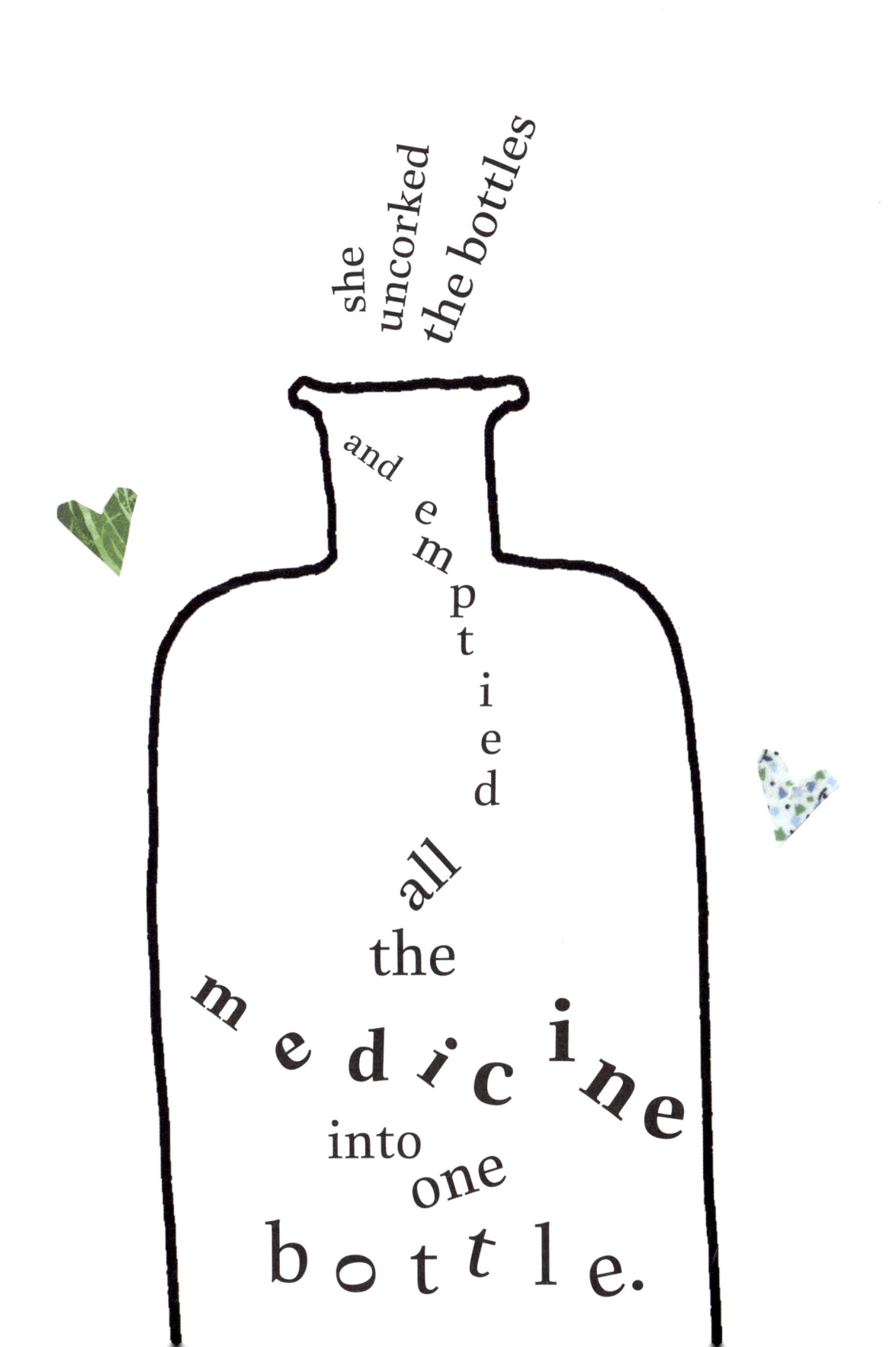

she uncorked the bottles and emptied all the medicine into one bottle.

She shook it hard. Then she put it to her mouth and gulped down huge mouthfuls. Annika, who knew some of the medicine should only be rubbed onto the skin, grew worried.

'But Pippi,' she said. 'How do you know the medicine isn't poisonous?'

'I'll find out,' said Pippi, gaily. 'I'll find out by tomorrow at the latest. If I'm still alive then it is *isn't* poisonous, and even the tiniest child can drink it.'

Tommy and Annika thought about this. After a while Tommy said, rather hesitantly and pessimistically:

'Yes, but what if it *is* poisonous, after all. What will happen then?'

'Then you can take what's left in the bottle and polish the dining-room furniture with it,' said Pippi. 'Poisonous or not, this **meducine** was still worth buying.'

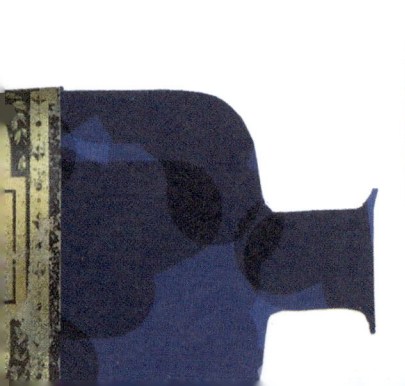

She picked up the bottle and put it in the trolley, alongside the false arm, Tommy's steam engine and air rifle, Annika's doll, and a bag of five small, red sweets. That was all that was left of the eighteen kilos. Mr Nilsson was sitting there, too. He was tired and wanted to ride.

'I'll tell you something, I think that was a really good **meducine**. I'm starting to feel brighter already. I'm especially feeling brighter and jollier in my tail,' Pippi said, wagging her bottom. Then off she went, pulling the trolley and wagging all the way home to Villa Villekulla. Tommy and Annika walked beside her and felt just the tiniest, tiniest twinge of a tummy ache.

Chapter Three
Pippi Writes a Letter and Goes to School —But Not for Long

'Today,' Tommy said, 'Annika and I have written to our granny.'

'Have you?' said Pippi, and she went on stirring the saucepan with the handle of her umbrella. 'I'm going to have a lovely dinner,' she went on, and stuck her nose down to smell. 'It says: "Cook for one hour, stirring vigorously, and serve immediately without ginger." What was that you said? You've written to your granny?'

'Yes,' answered Tommy, who was sitting on the log box dangling his legs. 'And very soon I expect we'll get an answer from her.'

'I never get any letters,' said Pippi, glumly.

'No, but you don't write any either,' said Annika. 'You can't get letters unless you write some yourself.'

'That's all because you won't go to school,' said Tommy. 'And you can't learn to write unless you go to school.'

'Of course I can write,' Pippi said. 'I know lots of different letters. Fridolf, a sailor on my dad's boat, taught me masses of writing. And when you get stuck with the writing, you can always turn to numbers. So, you see, I know all about writing! But I don't know what to write about. What do you usually put in letters?'

'Well,' said Tommy. 'First, I usually ask my granny how she is. Then I write something about the weather and that kind of thing. And today I told her I'd bashed a massive rat to death in our cellar.'

Pippi stirred and thought.

'It's a real shame I don't get any letters. Every other child gets letters. It simply can't go on like this. And if I haven't got a granny who can write to me, I might as well write to myself. I'll do it now, this very second.'

She opened the oven door and peered inside.

'There should be a pen in here, if I remember correctly.'

There was a pen in there. Pippi took it out. Then she tore a large, white paper bag in half and sat down at the kitchen table. Deep wrinkles appeared on her forehead and she looked as if she was concentrating hard.

'Now don't interrupt me, I'm thinking,' she said.

Tommy and Annika decided to pass the time by playing with Mr Nilsson. They took it in turns to dress him in his little suit and then take it off again. Annika also tried to lay him down in the green doll's bed where he usually slept. She wanted to play at being a nurse.

Tommy was to be the doctor and Mr Nilsson the sick child. But Mr Nilsson would insist on scrambling out of bed, scooting up the ceiling lamp and hanging there by his tail.

Pippi lifted her eyes from her writing.

'Silly Mr Nilsson,' she said. 'Sick children mustn't hang by their tail from the ceiling lamp. Not in this country, anyway. It goes on in South Africa, or so I've heard. There they hang up a child from the ceiling the minute it gets a temperature, and there it stays until it's better. But we're not in South Africa now, you might have noticed.

Eventually Tommy and Annika left Mr Nilsson alone and went to brush the horse. He was very happy when they went out to him on the veranda. He nosed their hands to see if they had any sugar cubes for him. They didn't, but Annika ran indoors and was soon back with a couple. Pippi wrote and wrote. At long last the letter was finished. She didn't have an envelope so Tommy ran home and fetched one for her. He gave her a stamp, too. Pippi wrote her name carefully on the envelope: Miss Pippilotta Longstocking, Villa Villekulla.

'What does the letter say?' asked Annika.

'How would I know?' answered Pippi. 'I haven't received it yet.'

Just then the postman walked past Villa Villekulla.

'Sometimes you're lucky enough to see a postman just when you need one,' Pippi said.

She ran out onto the road.

'Please take this letter to Pippi Longstocking, and look lively,' she said. 'It's urgent.'

The postman looked first at the letter and then at Pippi.

'Aren't you Pippi Longstocking?' he asked.

PIPPI WRITES A LETTER AND GOES TO SCHOOL
—BUT NOT FOR LONG

'Of course I am. Who did you think I was? The Duchess of Abyssinia?'

'Well then, why don't you take this letter yourself?' the postman said.

'Why don't I take it myself? Am *I* supposed to take it? Oh, that's going too far! Are people supposed to deliver their own letters these days? What have we got postmen for, in that case? We might just as well put them on the scrap heap straight away. I've never heard of anything so ridiculous. Oh no, my lad, carry on like this and you'll never get to be Postmaster General, believe me!'

The postman thought it was just as well to do as she wanted, so he went and posted the letter through Villa Villekulla's letterbox. It hardly had time to plop down on the doormat before Pippi eagerly picked it up.

'Oh, I can't wait to know what's in it,' she said. 'This is the first letter I've had in my life.'

All three children sat on the veranda steps and Pippi tore open the envelope. Tommy and Annika read over her shoulder. This is what the letter said:

4 PIPPI
YOU ARRNT ~~PORLY PORLEE~~ ILL ARR YOU?
WOT A PITEE IF YOU WAS ~~PORELEE~~ ILL
AS FOR ME
IM TOTTLY ALLRITE NUTHING RONG WITH THE WETHER EYETHER
YESTERDAY TOMEE BASHD A BIG RAT TO DETH
HE REELY DID
BEST WISHIZ FROM
PIPPI

'Oh,' said Pippi delightedly. 'My letter says exactly the same as the one you sent your granny, Tommy. That means I know it's a proper letter. I'll keep it safe as long as I live.'

She put the letter back in the envelope and then she put the envelope in one of the little drawers in the bureau in her sitting room. Looking at all the marvellous things stored in Pippi's bureau was about the best thing Tommy and Annika knew. Pippi was always giving them something as a little present, but even so the drawers never seemed to become empty.

PIPPI WRITES A LETTER AND GOES TO SCHOOL
—BUT NOT FOR LONG

'All the same,' said Tommy, after Pippi had hidden the letter. 'You made an awful lot of spelling mistakes.'

'Yes, you really should go to school and learn to write better,' said Annika.

'No thanks very much,' said Pippi. 'I did that for a whole day once and got so much learning stuffed into my head that it's still sploshing around in there.'

'But we're going on an outing any day now,' said Annika. 'The whole class.'

'Blow me down!' Pippi said, biting her plait. 'Would you believe it! And of course, I won't be allowed to come because I don't go to school! Seems some people think they can treat other people any way they like just because they haven't been to school and learnt multikipperation.'

'Multiplication,' Annika said, slowly and clearly.

'That's just what I said. **Multikipperation**.'

'We're going ever so far into the forest, ten whole kilometres. And we're going to stay there and play,' said Tommy.

'Blow me down,' said Pippi again.

The next day was so beautiful and warm that the children found it hard to sit still at their desks. The teacher opened all the windows and let the sun stream in. There was a silver birch tree just outside the school window and high up at the top sat a little starling. He was whistling so merrily that all Tommy and Annika and their school friends could do was listen to his song, and they didn't care at all about **9 x 9 = 81**.

All of a sudden Tommy jumped in astonishment.

'Look, Miss!' he shouted, pointing at the window. 'There's Pippi!'

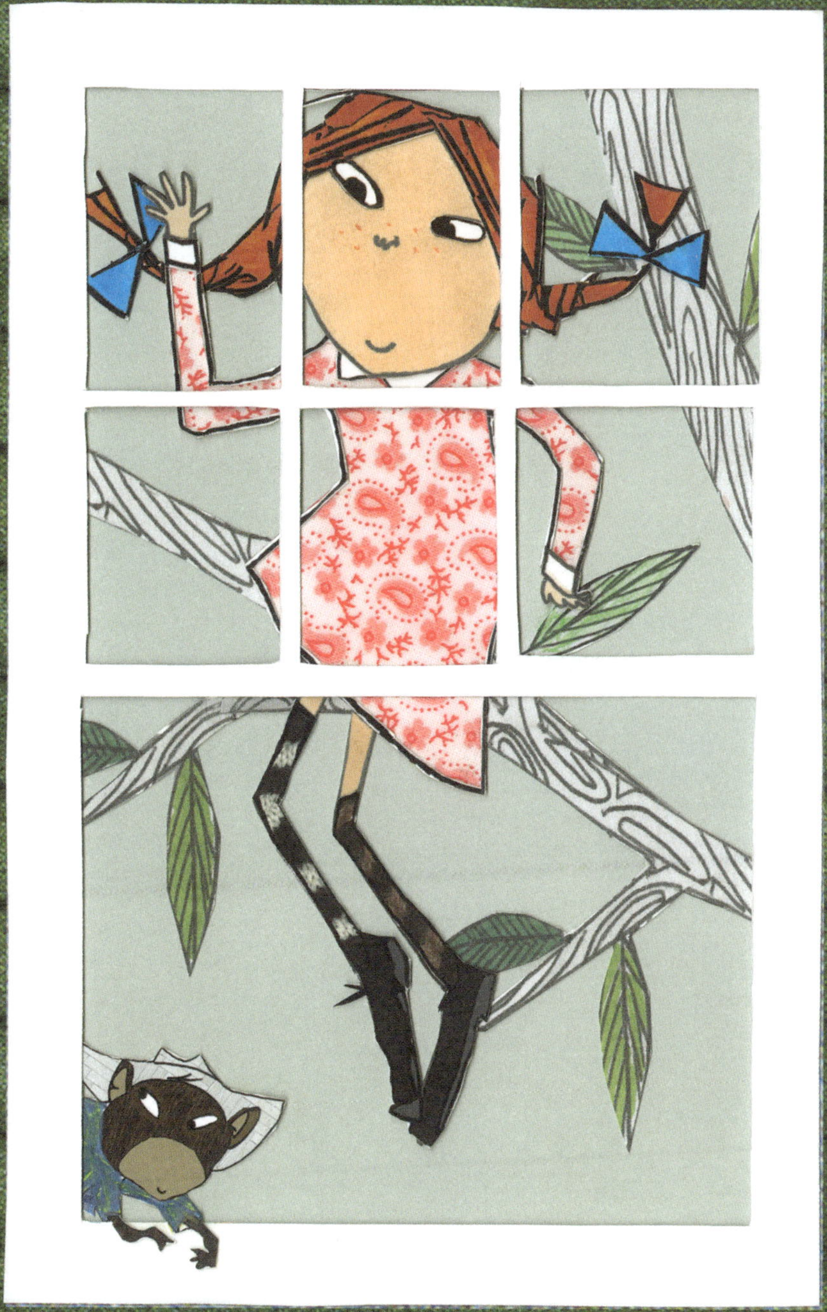

All the children's eyes turned in the same direction. And sure enough, there was Pippi, sitting on a branch in the birch tree. She was practically squashed up against the glass because the branch grew all the way to the window sill.

'Hello, Miss,' she called. 'Hello, kids!'

'Good morning, Pippi dear,' said the teacher. Pippi had spent a whole day at school once, so the teacher recognized her only too well. Pippi and the teacher had agreed that perhaps Pippi should come back to school when she was a little older and more sensible.

'What do you want, Pippi dear?'

'Oh, I thought I'd ask you to throw some **multikipperation** through the window,' said Pippi. 'Just enough to let me come on the outing. And if you've found any new letters, you can throw them out at the same time.'

'Would you like to come and join us for a while?' asked the teacher.

'I'd rather not,' Pippi replied bluntly, and leaned comfortably back against the branch. 'It only makes me dizzy. It's so stuffed full of knowledge in there you can cut it with a knife. But don't you think, Miss,' she went on, sounding hopeful, 'that a little bit of all that knowledge will fly out through the window and stick to me? Enough to let me go on the outing?'

'It's possible,' said the teacher, and she went back to her arithmetic lesson. The school children liked having Pippi in the tree outside. They had all been given sweets and toys by her the day she went shopping. Pippi had Mr Nilsson with her, naturally, and the children thought it was such fun watching him hurl himself from one branch to another. Occasionally he hopped down to the window too, and once he took a tremendous leap and landed on top of Tommy's head and started scratching his hair. But then the teacher told Pippi to call Mr Nilsson because Tommy was just about to work out what 315 divided by 7 was, and you can't do that with a monkey in your hair. Somehow the lesson was going all wrong. The spring sunshine, the starling, Pippi, and Mr Nilsson were too much for the children.

'I think you've all gone scatty,' the teacher said.

'You know what, Miss?' said Pippi from the tree outside. 'To be honest, I don't think this is a suitable day for **multikipperation**.'

'We're doing division,' said the teacher.

'You shouldn't be doing any kind of "shon" at all on a day like this,' said Pippi. 'Unless of course it's **jollificashon**.'

The teacher gave up.

'Perhaps you can provide the jollification, Pippi,' she said.

'Well, I'm not specially good at **jollificashon**,' Pippi said, hanging upside down by her knees, which made her red plaits almost drag on the ground. 'But I know a school where they have nothing else but **jollificashon**. "JOLLIFICASHON ALL DAY", the timetable says.'

'Oh, really?' said the teacher. 'And where is this school?'

'In Australia,' said Pippi. 'In a township. Down south.'

She sat on the branch and her eyes began to glow.

'What do they do when they have *jollificashon*?' asked the teacher.

'It varies,' said Pippi. 'Mostly they all leap out of the window together. Then they give a loud yell and rush

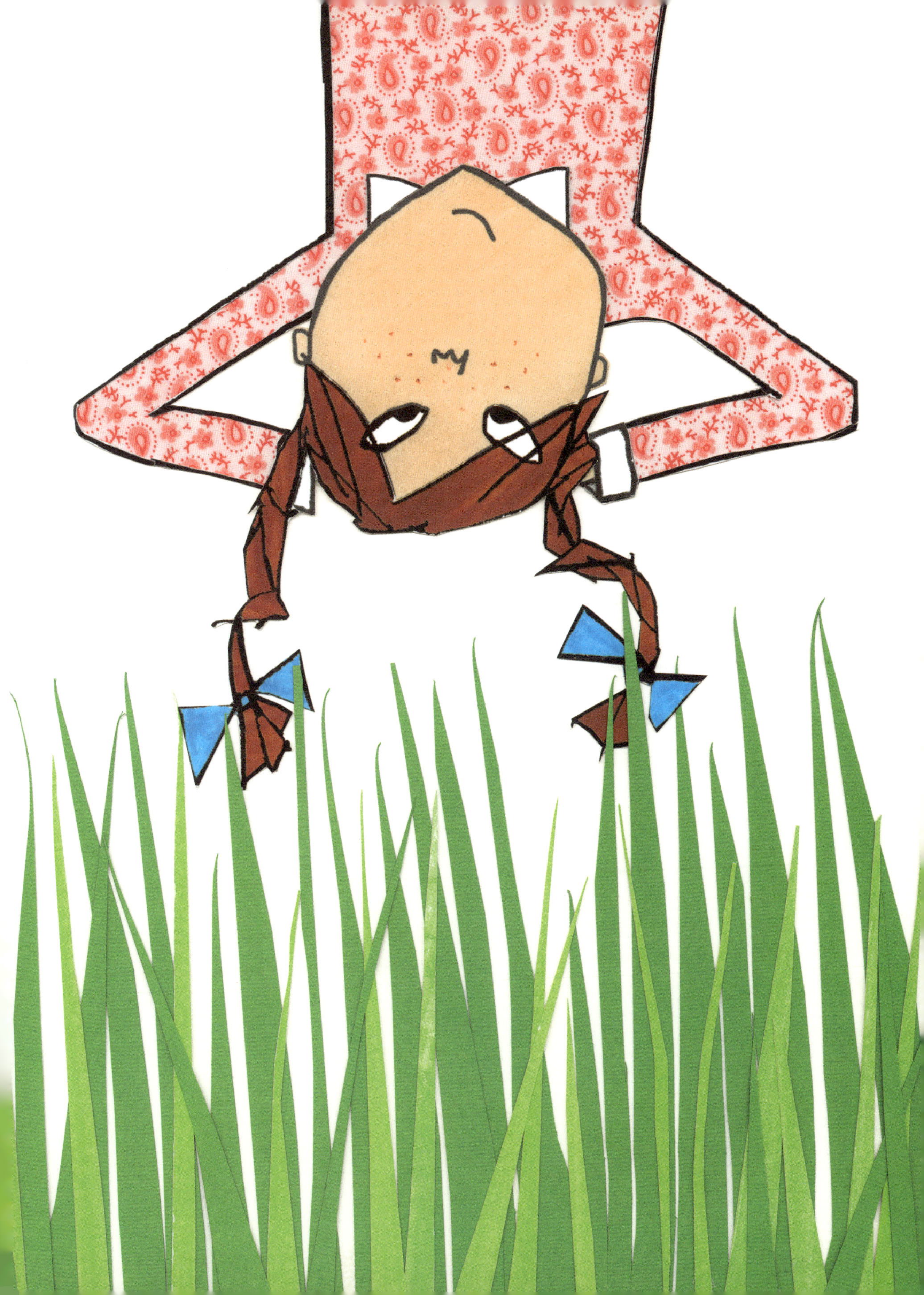

back into the classroom again and jump all over the benches until they drop.'

'But what does the teacher say when they do that?' asked the teacher.

'Oh, her,' said Pippi. 'She jumps around as well. Worse than anyone else. And then the children fight for about half an hour or so. The teacher stands and watches, cheering them on. If it's raining the children take off all their clothes, rush out into the rain and dance and leap about all over the place. The teacher plays a march on the school organ, so they can keep in time. Some of them stand under the drainpipe and get a proper soaking.'

'Do they, indeed?' said the teacher.

'I should say so,' said Pippi. 'It's an awfully good school. One of the best they've got in Australia. But it is a long way south.'

'No doubt,' said the teacher. 'But I don't think we'll be having quite so much fun in this school.'

'Pity,' said Pippi. 'If it was only a question of jumping around on benches then I think I'd come in for a while.'

PIPPI WRITES A LETTER AND GOES TO SCHOOL
—BUT NOT FOR LONG

'The jumping will have to wait until we have the outing,' said the teacher.

'Can I really come?' shouted Pippi, and she was so happy she turned a backwards somersault out of the tree. 'Then I'll definitely be writing to Australia to tell them. They can have as much **jollificashon** they like as far as I'm concerned. Because an outing is *much* more fun.'

Chapter Four
Pippi Goes

There was the sound of many feet tramping along the road and much chattering and laughter. Here was Tommy with his backpack and Annika in her brand new summer dress, and their teacher and all their classmates, apart from one poor thing who had a sore throat on the very day of the outing. And there, out in front, rode Pippi on her horse. Behind her sat Mr Nilsson, holding his little mirror. He was reflecting sunbeams with it and looked more than satisfied when he aimed one right in Tommy's eyes.

Annika had been absolutely sure it would rain on this

on the School Outing

particular day. She had been so sure that she was almost angry in advance. But just think what luck you can have sometimes—nothing could stop the sun from shining even though it was the day of the outing, and Annika's heart leapt for joy as she walked along the road in her pretty new dress. In fact, all the children looked very happy and keen. The roadside was thick with pussy willow and in one place they came across a field full of cowslips. Every child decided to pick an armful of pussy willow and a bunch of cowslips—on the way home.

'Such a lovely, lovely day,' sighed Annika, and looked

up at Pippi sitting on her horse as straight-backed as a general.

'Yes, I haven't had this much fun since I fought that heavy-weight boxer in San Francisco,' said Pippi. 'Do you want to ride for a little while?'

Annika certainly did, so Pippi lifted her up to sit in front of her on the horse. But when the other children saw that, they wanted to ride as well, of course. And so they did. They took turns, although Tommy and Annika were allowed to ride just a *little* bit longer than the others. One of the girls was having trouble with blisters. She was allowed to sit behind Pippi and ride the whole way. But Mr Nilsson pulled her plaits whenever he got the chance.

The destination of the outing was a forest called Moon Star Forest, but the children always called it "Monster Forest". When they were almost there Pippi jumped down from the saddle, patted her horse and said: 'You've been carrying us for such a long way, now it's your turn to be tired. You shouldn't be the only one doing all the work.'

With that she lifted up the horse on her strong arms

and carried him all the way until they came to a little glade in the forest where the teacher told them to stop. Pippi looked around and called out:

'Come on, all you monsters, let's see who's the strongest!'

But the teacher explained to Pippi that Monster Forest didn't mean there were actual monsters in the forest. Pippi was very disappointed.

'A monster forest with no monsters! What will people think of next! Soon they'll be having a bonfire without flames, or dances round a Christmas tree without the Christmas tree! Just to save money! But the day they start having sweet shops without sweets is the day I'll go and have a sharp word with them. Ho hum, I'll just have to be a monster myself, there's no other way.'

She let out such a fearsome roar that the teacher had to cover her ears and several of the children trembled in fear.

'Yes, let's pretend Pippi's a monster!' shouted Tommy joyfully, and clapped his hands. All the children thought it was a good suggestion. The monster went and hid inside a deep crack in the rocks, where it had its den, and the children ran about outside and teased it, calling:

'Silly, silly monster! Silly, silly monster!'

Then the monster came rushing out, yelling at the top of its voice and chasing the children, who ran off in all directions to hide. Those who were caught were dragged back to the den and the monster said it would cook them for dinner. But sometimes they managed to escape while the monster was out chasing more children. To do that they had to climb up the crack in the rock, and that was really hard. There was only a small pine tree to hang onto and it was tricky knowing where to put their feet. But it was exciting and the children thought it was the best game they had ever played. Their teacher sat in the green grass and read a book, glancing up at the children from time to time.

PIPPI GOES ON THE SCHOOL OUTING

'That certainly is the wildest monster I have ever seen,' she muttered to herself.

It certainly was. The monster hopped and yelled and threw three boys over its shoulder and dragged them off to its den. Sometimes it climbed at lightning speed up the highest tree and bounded from branch to branch just like a monkey, and sometimes it threw itself up on its horse and caught up with some children who were trying to escape among the trees. When the horse came galloping up the monster bent down in the saddle, grabbed the children as it hurtled past, threw them up in front of her on the horse and made a beeline back to its den, bellowing:

'Now I'm going to

cook you for my dinner!'

It was such fun the children didn't want to stop. But all of a sudden it went absolutely quiet and still, and when Tommy and Annika came running over to see what was going on, the monster was sitting on a rock with a very odd expression on its face and looking at something it was holding in its hand.

'It's dead. Look, it's all dead,' said the monster.

The dead thing was a baby bird. It had fallen out of its nest and been killed.

'Oh, what a shame,' said Annika. The monster nodded.

'Pippi, you're crying,' Tommy blurted out.

'Crying—me?' said Pippi. 'I'm not crying at all.'

'But your eyes are all red,' insisted Tommy.

'Are my eyes red?' said Pippi, and she borrowed Mr Nilsson's mirror to have a look. 'Call these red eyes? You should have been with me and Dad in Batavia! There was a man there who had such red eyes the police ordered him not to go out on the street.'

'Why?' Tommy asked.

'Because people thought he was a stop light, see? And the traffic ground to a halt wherever he walked. Red eyes—me! No, you mustn't think I'm crying over this scraggy little thing,' Pippi said.

'Silly, silly monster! Silly, silly monster!'

Children came running up from all around to see where the monster had got to. Then the monster took the scraggy little bird away and lay it very gently on a bed of soft moss.

'If I could I would make you alive again,' she said with a deep sigh. Then she let out a terrifying howl.

'Now I'm going to cook you for my dinner!' she shouted, and with joyful screams the children disappeared among the bushes.

One of the girls in the class—Ulla, her name was—lived in a house very close to Monster Forest. Ulla's mum had promised that she could invite her teacher and her classmates, and Pippi too, of course, for refreshments in their garden. So after the children had played the monster game long enough and climbed on the rocks for a while and sailed bark boats in a pool and seen who had dared to jump from a high rock, Ulla said she thought it was about time they went back to her house to drink orange squash. And their teacher, who had read her book from cover to cover, agreed.

She gathered the children together in a large flock and they left Monster Forest.

Out on the road a man was coming along with a cartload of sacks. They were very heavy sacks and there were a lot of them, and the horse was old and tired. All at once one of the cartwheels drove down into the ditch. The man, whose name was Blomsterlund, by the way, flew into a dreadful fit of rage. He thought it was the horse's fault. He took out his whip and moments later stinging lashes were raining down on the horse's back. The horse pulled and strained and tried with all its strength to get the load back onto the road again, but it couldn't. Blomsterlund grew even angrier and he whipped the horse even harder. It was then the teacher noticed what was happening, and she became very distressed and was filled with pity for the horse.

'How can you even think of whipping a creature that way!' she said to Blomsterlund. Blomsterlund stopped whipping for a moment and spat before answering.

'Don't meddle in things that don't concern you,' he said. 'Otherwise I just might let you feel the whip as well, all of you.'

He spat again.

And he raised the whip again.

The poor horse was quivering all over.

Then it was as if a bolt of lightning came shooting through the flock of children.

It was Pippi.

Her nose was completely white. And when Pippi's nose was white it meant she was angry, Annika and Tommy knew that.

She rushed straight at Blomsterlund, grabbed him round the waist and threw him high into the air.

When he came down she caught him and threw him up again.

Four times, five times, six times he made a little flying trip.

Blomsterlund had no idea what was going on.

'Help, help!' he yelled, frantically. Eventually he landed with a thud on the road. He had dropped the whip. Pippi stood in front of him with her hands on her hips.

'You'll never, ever beat that horse again,' she told him sternly. 'Never, is that understood? Once in Cape Town I met a man and he beat his horse too. He wore such a fine uniform, that fellow, and I told him that if he beat his horse again I would beat him until there wasn't a thread left of his fine uniform. And guess what? One week later, he was beating his horse again! Shame about such a nice uniform.'

Blomsterlund sat where he was, totally bewildered.

'Where are you taking that load?' asked Pippi.

Frightened, Blomsterlund pointed to a cottage that lay a short distance down the road.

'There, back home,' he said.

Then Pippi unfastened the horse. It was still trembling from exhaustion and fear.

'There, there, little Neddy,' she said. 'Things will change around here, believe you me!'

And she lifted him up in her strong arms and

carried him home to his stable. The horse looked as astonished as Blomsterlund.

The children and their teacher waited on the road for Pippi. And Blomsterlund stood by his loaded cart and scratched his head. He didn't know how he was going to get it home. Then back Pippi came. She lifted off one of the heavy sacks and loaded it onto Blomsterlund's back.

'There we go,' she said. 'Let's see if you're as clever at carrying as you are at whipping.'

Pippi took the whip.

'You know, I really should give you a little taste of this whip, since you're so keen on it. But it seems to be broken,' she said, snapping off a piece. 'Completely, totally broken, sad to say,' she said, and snapped the whip into tiny, tiny pieces.

Blomsterlund trudged off with the sack without saying a word. He could only pant and puff. And Pippi took hold of the shafts and pulled the cart home for Blomsterlund.

'Might as well, it costs nothing,' she said, as she left the cart outside Blomsterlund's stable. 'I was more than happy to do it. Your flying trips are free, too.'

Then she walked off. Blomsterlund stood for a long time, watching her go.

'Hooray for Pippi!' shouted the children when Pippi came back. Their teacher was also very pleased with Pippi and congratulated her.

'That was the right thing to do,' she said. 'People should be kind to animals. And to other people too, of course.'

Pippi sat on her horse, looking very satisfied with herself.

'I was certainly good to Blomsterlund, leastways,' she said. 'All those free flying trips!'

'That's what we are here for,' the teacher said. 'To be friendly and kind to other people.'

Pippi stood on her head on her horse and waggled her legs.

'Ha, ha,' she said. 'What are other people here for, then?'

In Ulla's garden a large table was laid ready for them. There were so many biscuits and buns the children's mouths watered and they raced to sit down round the table. Pippi chose to sit at the short end. The first thing she did was cram two buns into her mouth at once. She looked like one of those cherubs in church, with cheeks like balls.

'Pippi, it's normal to wait until you have been asked to begin,' the teacher said, reprovingly.

'No shtanding on sheremony for my shake,' Pippi managed to say through the buns. 'I'm not sho fushy about following roolsh.'

At that moment Ulla's mum walked over to her with a jug of juice in one hand and a jug of hot chocolate in the other.

'Juice or hot chocolate?' she asked.

'Joosh *and* shocolate,' said Pippi. 'I want joosh on one bun and shocolate on the other.'

And without asking she took the jugs from Ulla's mother and took a large gulp from each of them.

'She's been at sea all her life,' the teacher whispered by way of explanation to Ulla's mother, who was looking rather astonished.

'I see,' said Ulla's mother, and she decided to ignore Pippi's bad manners.

'Are you going to have a ginger biscuit?' she said, holding out a plate to Pippi.

'It looks like it,' Pippi said, giggling at her own joke. 'They're not terribly pretty, but I hope they taste good anyway,' she said, taking a fistful. Then she caught sight of some very pretty pink cakes further down the table. She gave Mr Nilsson's tail a gentle tug and said to him:

'Hey, Mr Nilsson, toddle over and get some of those pink thingummies for me. Take a couple or three while you're at it!'

And Mr Nilsson scuttled straight down the table, bumping into the glasses and making the drink splash out.

'I hope you're full up now,' said Ulla's mother, when Pippi went to thank her afterwards.

'Hmm, not full up, but thirsty,' Pippi said, scratching her ear.

'Well, we didn't have an awful lot to offer you,' said Ulla's mother.

'No, but it could have been worse,' said Pippi, in a friendly way.

That's when the teacher decided to take Pippi aside and teach her about manners.

'Listen to me, Pippi dear,' she said, kindly. 'You do want to be a fine lady when you grow up, don't you?'

'You mean one of those with a veil over her nose and three chins underneath?'

'I mean a lady who always knows how to behave and is polite and well-brought-up. A really fine lady. You want to be like that, don't you?'

'It's worth considering,' said Pippi. 'But you see, Miss, I have sort of already decided to be a pirate when I grow up.'

She thought for a moment.

'But don't you think, Miss, that someone can be a pirate and a Very Fine Lady at the same time? Because in that case . . .'

The teacher didn't think so.

'Oh dear, oh dear, what shall I decide to be then?' Pippi said, miserably.

The teacher said that whatever path Pippi took in life, it wouldn't hurt her to learn some manners. You simply couldn't behave the way Pippi had done at the table just now.

'To think it should be so complicated to learn How To Behave,' sighed Pippi. 'Can't you simply tell me the most important rules?'

The teacher did her best. She explained to Pippi, and Pippi listened attentively. You mustn't help yourself unless invited. No more than one cake at a time. Don't eat from your knife. Don't scratch yourself while talking to other people, don't do this, don't do that. Pippi nodded, thinking hard.

'I'll get up an hour earlier every day and practise,' she said. 'Then I'll have the knack, in case I decide not to be a pirate.'

A short distance away Annika was sitting on the lawn. She was lost in thought with a finger stuck up her nose.

'Annika,' called Pippi, sternly. 'What are you thinking of? Remember, a Very Fine Lady only picks her nose when she's alone!'

But then the teacher said it was time to pack up

and march home. All the children lined up. Only Pippi was left sitting on the lawn. She had a concentrated expression on her face as if she was listening to something.

'What's up, Pippi dear?' asked the teacher.

'Well, Miss,' said Pippi. 'Can a Very Fine Lady's tummy rumble?'

She sat in silence, still concentrating.

'Because if it *can't*, I might just as well decide here and now to be a pirate.'

Chapter Five
Pippi and Market Day

The tiny little town had a market day. Once a year they had their market, and each time all the children of the town were giddy with joy that something so nice could be happening. On that day the little town didn't look at all like it usually did. Crowds of people were swarming everywhere, flags were flying and the square was filled with stalls selling the most wonderful things. There was such a hubbub and commotion that simply walking along the streets was exciting. And best of all, on the edge of town was a huge funfair with a carousel and rifle ranges and a travelling theatre and every possible kind of entertainment. Including a menagerie. A menagerie containing all the wild animals you could think of—tigers, giant snakes, monkeys and sea lions. You could stand outside the menagerie and hear strange growlings and howlings, such as you have never heard before in your entire life. And of course, if you had the money you could also go in and see it all.

So it wasn't surprising that the bow in Annika's hair was positively shaking from excitement as Annika stood dressed and ready on market day morning, or that Tommy practically swallowed his cheese sandwich whole in his hurry. Tommy and Annika's mum asked if they would like to go to the market with her, but Tommy and Annika squirmed and said if their mum didn't mind they would really rather go with Pippi.

'Because, you see,' Tommy explained to Annika as they slipped through the gate to Villa Villekulla, 'I think when we're with Pippi more exciting things happen, somehow.'

Annika thought so too.

Pippi was standing dressed and ready in the middle of the kitchen, waiting for them. She had finally found her hat that was the size of a cartwheel. It had been in the wood shed.

'I forgot I used it to carry logs in the other day,' she said, pulling it down over her forehead. 'Don't I look smart?'

Tommy and Annika couldn't deny it. Pippi had blackened her eyebrows with ashes from the fire and painted her lips and nails red. And she had also put on a very lovely ball gown that reached down to the floor. It was cut low at the back, showing her red vest. From under the hem her long black shoes poked out,

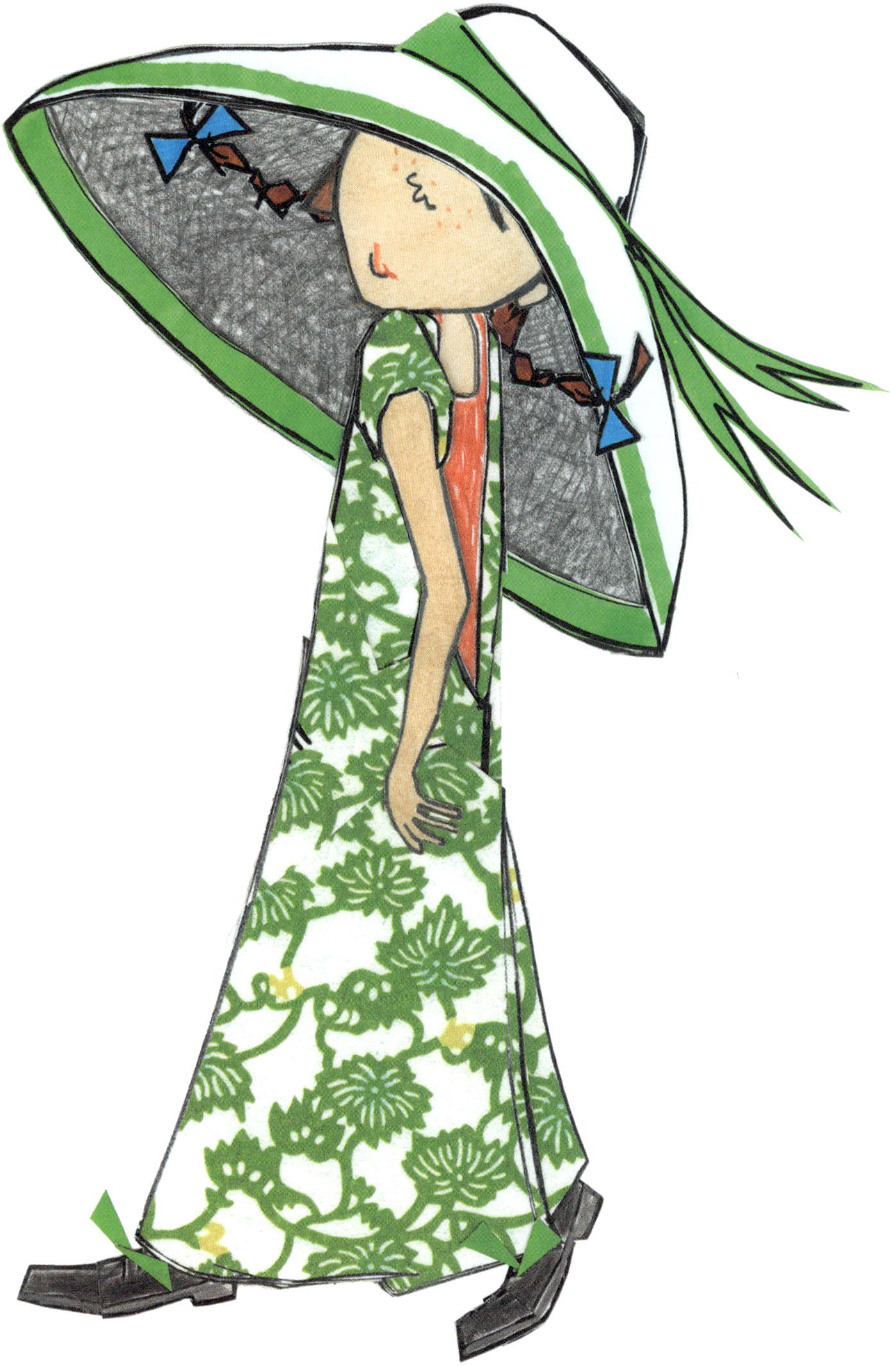

and they were even smarter than usual because she had tied them with the green ribbons she used for special occasions.

'I think it's important to look like a Very Grand Lady when you go to a market day,' she said, strutting along the road as elegantly as it is possible to do in such large shoes. She hitched up the skirt of her dress and said in a voice totally unlike her own:

'Delightful! Delightful!'

'What's delightful?' asked Tommy.

'Me,' said Pippi smugly.

Tommy and Annika thought *everything* was delightful on market day. It was delightful being jostled by the crowds in the streets and going from one stall to another in the square, looking at all the things on display. Pippi bought a red silk handkerchief for Annika as a market day gift, and Tommy got a cap, the kind he had always wanted but his mum didn't want him to have. From another stall Pippi bought two bell shapes made of glass and crammed with small pink and white sweets.

'Oh, Pippi, you're so kind!' said Annika, clutching her glass bell.

'Oh yes, delightful,' said Pippi, hitching up her dress again.

A stream of people was making its way towards the toll gates. Pippi, Tommy, and Annika followed it.

'What a hullaballoo,' Tommy said. He was ecstatic. The barrel organ was playing, the carousel was going round, people were shouting and laughing. Dart-throwing and crockery-smashing was in full swing. People were crowding round the shooting ranges, anxious to show their skill at hitting the bullseye.

'I'd like to have a closer look at that,' said Pippi, and she pulled Tommy and Annika over to one of the shooting ranges. At that precise moment there was no one waiting at this particular shooting range, and the woman who handed out the rifles and took the money looked pretty fed-up. Three little kids were not what she would call customers. She took absolutely no notice of them. Pippi studied the target with interest. It was made of cardboard and looked like a large figure of a man in a blue coat and with a face as round as a ball. Right in the middle of the face was a red nose. That was the bullseye, where you had to aim. If you weren't lucky enough to hit the nose you had to try and hit somewhere close to it, at least. Shots that didn't hit the face counted as misses.

Eventually the woman grew tired of the children standing there. She wanted customers who would spend money to shoot.

'Are you still hanging around?' she said, irritably.

'Nope, we're sitting in the town square cracking nuts,' Pippi replied.

'What are you gawking at?' said the lady, even more irritably. 'Are you waiting for someone to come and start shooting?'

'Nope. We're waiting for you to start turning somersaults,' said Pippi.

But just then a customer did turn up, a fine gentleman with a gold watch and chain across his stomach. He picked up a rifle and weighed it in his hand.

'Perhaps I'll shoot a few rounds, just to show you how it's done,' he said.

He looked about him to see if he had an audience. But there was no one there apart from Pippi, Tommy, and Annika.

PIPPI AND MARKET DAY

'Watch this, kids,' he said. 'You will now have your first demonstration in the art of hitting a target. This is how you do it.'

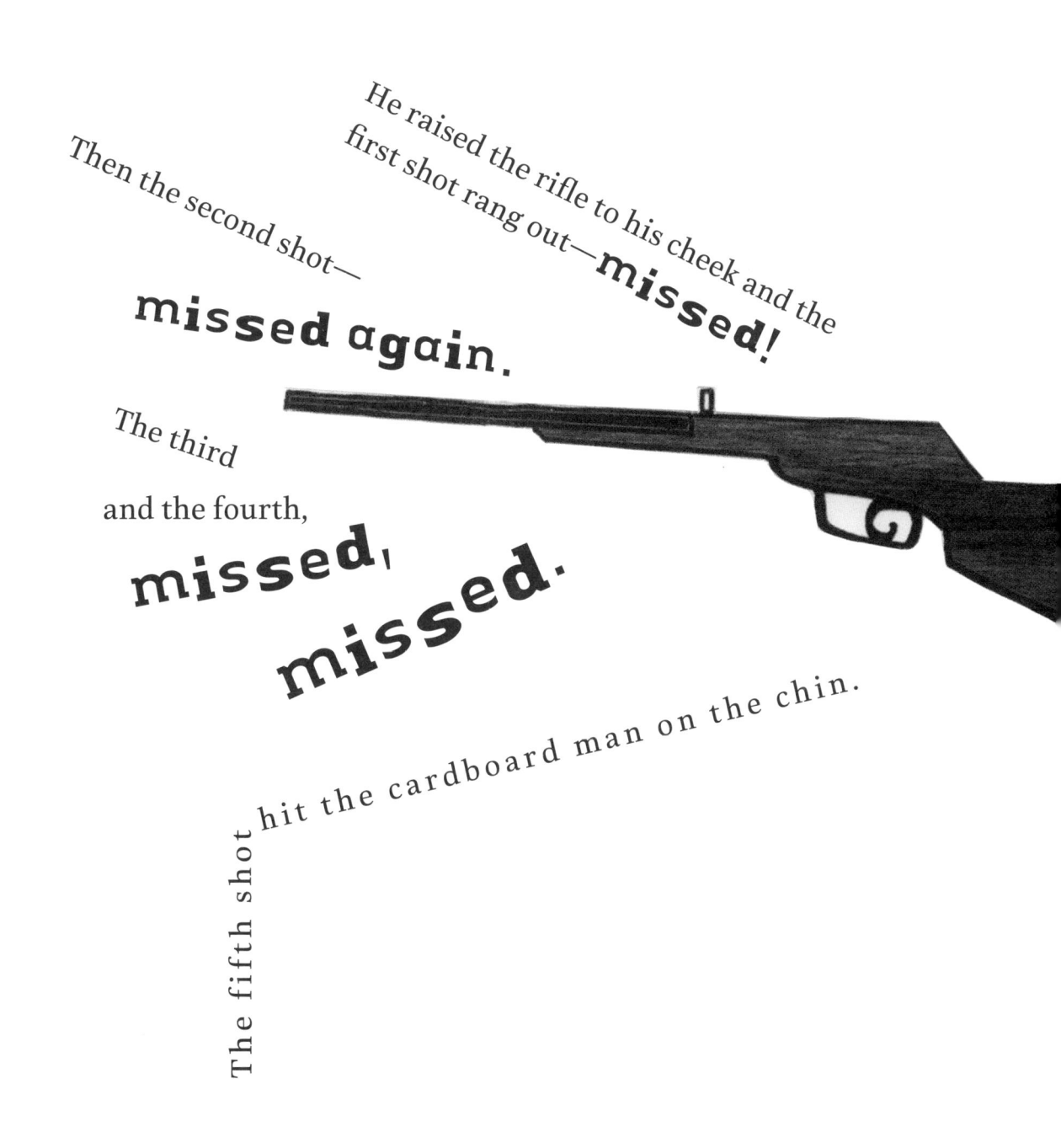

He raised the rifle to his cheek and the first shot rang out— **missed!**

Then the second shot— **missed again.**

The third

and the fourth, **missed, missed.**

The fifth shot hit the cardboard man on the chin.

'Useless rifle,' said the fine gentleman angrily, and threw down the weapon. Pippi picked it up and loaded it.

'Oh, how clever you are, sir,' she said. 'Next time I'll do it *exactly* the way you showed us, and not like this!'

Bam, bam, bam, bam, **BAM!**

Five shots hit the cardboard man slap in the middle of his nose. Pippi handed the rifle-range lady a golden coin and walked away.

The carousel was so indescribably splendid that Tommy and Annika gasped in amazement when they saw it. There were black and white and brown horses you could sit on. Their manes were real and they looked almost alive, and they had saddles and reins too. And you were allowed to choose whichever horse you wanted. Pippi bought tickets for one whole golden coin and got so many in return they hardly fitted in her large purse.

'If I'd handed over another golden coin I expect they'd have given me the whole **whirlygig-thingummy**,' she said to Tommy and Annika, who stood waiting for her.

Tommy picked a black horse and Annika chose a

white one. Pippi sat Mr Nilsson on a black horse that looked terribly fierce. Mr Nilsson immediately started rummaging through its mane for fleas.

'Is Mr Nilsson also going on the carousel?' Annika asked, in astonishment.

'Naturally,' said Pippi. 'If I'd thought about it I'd have brought my own horse along too. He could do with some entertainment. And a horse riding on another horse—that would have been something extra special in the horse world.'

Pippi herself leaped onto the saddle of a brown horse and the next second the carousel was off, as the steam organ played "Do You Recall the Happy Memories of our Childhood Days?".

It was wonderful riding on the carousel, thought Annika and Tommy. Pippi also looked as if she was enjoying herself. She was standing on her head on the horse with her legs sticking up in the air and her long ballgown tumbling down around her shoulders. The people watching beside the carousel could only see a red vest and a pair of green bloomers, along with Pippi's long thin legs with one brown and one black stocking, and her long black shoes jauntily waggling up and down.

'That's how a Very Fine Lady rides on a carousel,' Pippi said, when the first ride came to an end.

For a whole hour the children rode the carousel, but eventually Pippi was so cross-eyed she was seeing three carousels instead of one.

'And that makes it hard to decide which one to go on,' she said. 'So I think we'll move on.'

She had stacks of tickets left so she gave them to a few little children who were standing there watching. They hadn't even had one ride on the carousel because they didn't have any money to pay for it.

Outside a nearby tent stood a man yelling:

'Next performance in two minutes. Don't miss the stupendous drama, "Murder of the Countess Aurora" or, "Who's that skulking in the bushes?"'

'If someone's skulking in the bushes we've got to find out who it is, and fast,' said Pippi. 'Come on, let's go in.'

Pippi walked up to the ticket window.

'Can I go in for half price if I promise to look with only one eye?' she asked, in a sudden fit of thriftiness.

But the lady in the ticket window wouldn't hear of it.

'I can't see any bushes or anyone lurking in them either,' Pippi said crossly, after she and Tommy and Annika had sat themselves down in the front row, closest to the curtain.

'It hasn't started yet,' Tommy said.

At that moment the curtain went up and there was Countess Aurora, pacing up and down the stage. She was wringing her hands and looking very anxious. Pippi followed it all very closely.

'She's sad and no mistake,' she said to Tommy and Annika. 'Either that or she's got a safety pin sticking in her somewhere.'

The Countess Aurora *was* sad. She rolled her eyes to the roof and wailed:

'Was anyone ever as unlucky as I? My children taken from me, my husband vanished, myself encompassed by villains and bandits who want to kill me.'

'Oh, that's terrible to hear!' said Pippi, and looked quite red around the eyes.

'How I wish I were already dead!' said Countess Aurora.

Then Pippi burst into floods of tears.

'Oh no, please don't say that,' she sobbed. 'Things will get better. Your children will be all right and you'll find a new chap. There are so many ch-a-a-ps,' she hiccupped between the sobs.

But up marched the theatre manager—he was the man who had been standing outside the tent, shouting—and told Pippi that if she couldn't sit in absolute silence she must leave the theatre instantly.

'I'll try,' said Pippi, rubbing her eyes.

It was a tremendously thrilling play. Tommy sat there crumpling his hat in his hands, he was so nervous, and Annika squeezed her hands together tight. Pippi's eyes were shining and she didn't take them off the Countess for a second. Things went from bad to worse for the poor Countess. There she was, walking around the palace garden, minding her own business, when suddenly there was a cry. It was Pippi. She had caught sight of a man standing behind a tree and he didn't look very nice. It seemed the Countess Aurora had also heard something rustling, because she said in a petrified voice:

'Who is that, lurking in the bushes?'

'I can tell you!' said Pippi, eagerly. 'It's a pesky scoundrel with a black moustache! Run into the woodshed and lock the door, smartish!'

Back came the theatre manager and told Pippi to remove herself immediately.

'What, and leave the Countess alone with a good-for-nothing like him? You don't know me, in that case,' Pippi said.

On the stage the play continued. Suddenly the nasty man in the bushes came rushing out and threw himself over Countess Aurora.

'Ha ha, your last moment has come,' he hissed between clenched teeth.

'We'll see about that,' said Pippi, and with a jump she was on the stage. She gripped the villain around the waist and hurled him down among the seats. She was still crying.

'How could you?' she sobbed. 'What have you got against the Countess anyway? Remember, her children and husband have gone and she's all al-o-o-ne!'

She went over to the Countess, who had feebly collapsed onto a garden bench.

'You can come and live with me in Villa Villekulla if you like,' she said, to comfort her.

Howling at the top of her lungs Pippi stumbled out of the theatre, closely followed by Tommy and Annika. And the theatre manager. He shook his fists at her. But the audience applauded and thought it had been a really good show.

Outside, Pippi blew her nose on her frock and said:

'We've got to cheer ourselves up now, that's for sure. That was far too sad.'

'The menagerie,' Tommy said. 'We haven't been to the menagerie.'

So that's where they went. But first they went to the sandwich stall and Pippi bought six sandwiches for them each and three bottles of lemonade.

'Because crying always makes me hungry,' said Pippi.

Inside the menagerie there was plenty to look at. One elephant and two tigers in a cage and several sea lions that could toss a ball to each other, masses of monkeys and a hyena, and two enormous snakes. Pippi immediately took Mr Nilsson to the monkey cage so that he could say hello to his relations. Inside sat a very gloomy chimpanzee.

'Come along, Mr Nilsson,' said Pippi. 'Say hello nicely! I imagine this is your grandfather's cousin's auntie's uncle's little third cousin!'

Mr Nilsson lifted his straw hat and greeted the chimpanzee as politely as he knew how. But the chimpanzee didn't bother greeting him back.

Both the enormous snakes lay in a large box. Once an hour they were taken out by the beautiful snake charmer Fräulein Paula, who displayed them from a platform. The children were in luck. There was to be a display that very minute. Annika was terrified of snakes. She held a firm grip on Pippi's arm. Fräulein Paula held up one of the snakes, a great big ugly thing, and draped it round her neck like a feather boa.

'It appears to be a boa constrictor,' Pippi whispered to Tommy and Annika. 'I wonder what sort the other one is.'

She walked over to the box and took out the other snake. This one was even bigger and uglier than the first one. Pippi draped it around her neck just like Fräulein Paula had done. All the people in the menagerie screamed in fright. Fräulein Paula threw her snake into the box and dashed over to try and save Pippi from certain death. The sudden commotion made Pippi's snake angry and afraid, and for the life of him he couldn't understand why he was draped around the neck of a red-haired girl instead of Fräulein Paula, like he usually was. He made up his mind to give the red-haired girl a bite to remember him by, and he squeezed his body around her in a tight grip, strong enough to crush an ox.

'Don't try that old trick on me,' Pippi said. 'I've seen much bigger snakes, believe you me. In Furthest India.'

She pulled the snake off her and put him back in his box. Tommy and Annika stood there looking as white as ghosts.

'That was a boa constrictor as well,' said Pippi, hoisting up one of her stockings. 'Exactly as I suspected.'

Fräulein Paula scolded them for a long time in some kind of foreign language, while all the people in the menagerie breathed a sigh of relief. But they had sighed too early because apparently this was a day filled with all sorts of events. Afterwards nobody quite knew how it happened. The tigers had just been fed a large red piece of meat and the animal keeper said he was sure he had shut the door securely behind him. But a moment later a terrified cry rang out:

'There's a tiger on the loose!'

And so there was. There he lay, the yellow-striped beast, curled up outside the menagerie and ready to lunge. People fled in all directions. But one little girl stood trapped in a corner right beside the tiger.

'Keep absolutely still!' people shouted at her. They hoped the tiger would leave her alone if she didn't move.

'What shall we do?' wailed the people, nervously wringing their hands.

'Phone the police,' someone said.

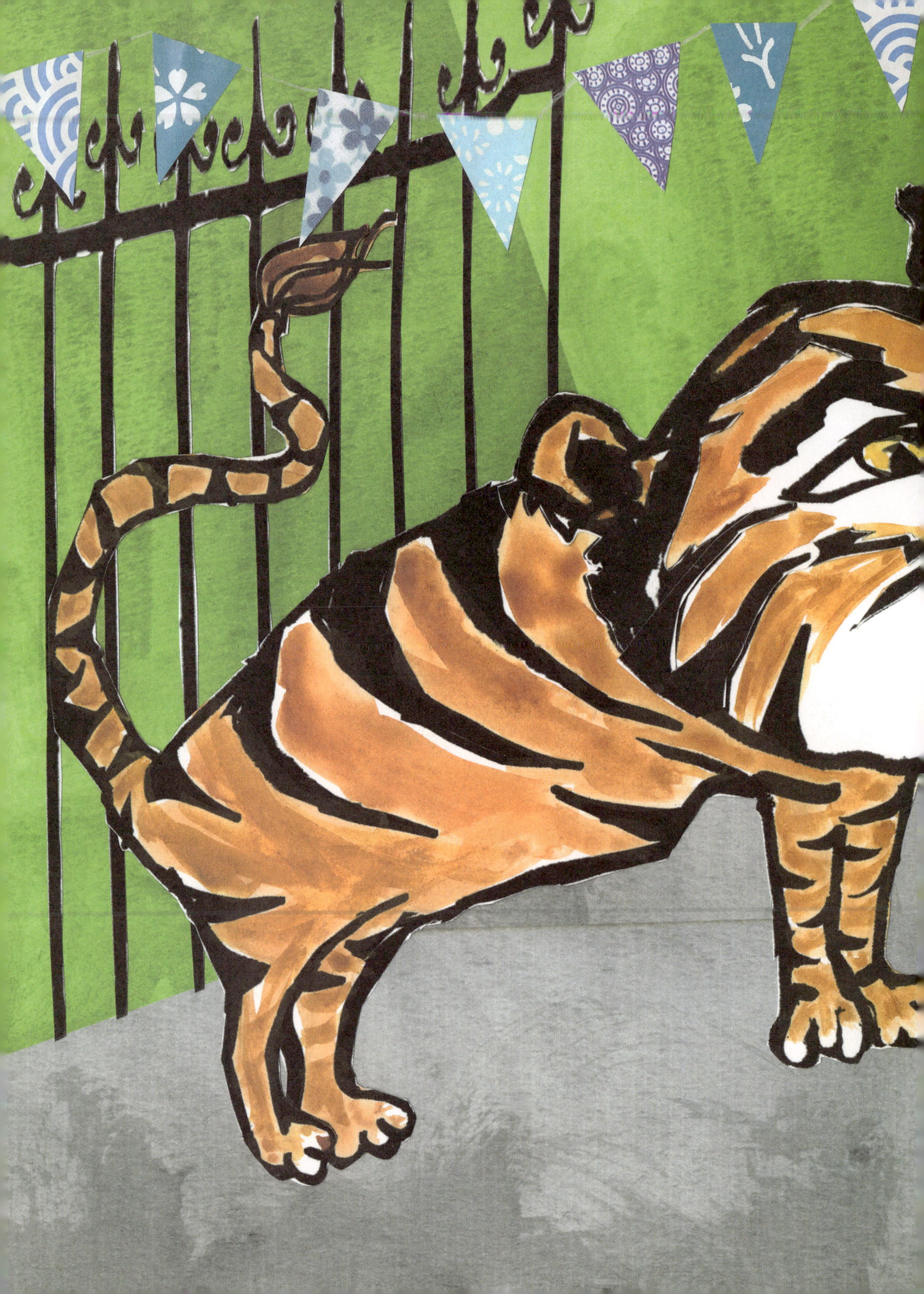

'Call the fire brigade,' suggested someone else.
'Get Pippi Longstocking,' said Pippi, and stepped forward. She crouched down a few metres from the tiger and called him to her.
'Here kitty, kitty!'

The tiger gave a horrendous roar and bared his **terrifying teeth.**

Pippi raised a warning finger.

'Bite me and I'll bite you back, trust me,' she said.

Then the tiger leaped right at her.

'What's up? Can't you take a little joke?' Pippi said, and threw him off her. With a loud growl that gave everyone goose bumps, the tiger leaped at Pippi again. This time it was clear he wanted to bite her head off.

'Have it your own way,' Pippi said. 'But remember, you started it!'

With one hand she clamped the tiger's jaws shut and then she carried him tenderly in her arms back to his cage, all the while humming a little tune:

'Pussy cat, pussy cat, where have you been?'

Then everyone breathed a sigh of relief for the second time, and the little girl who had been stuck in the corner ran to her mummy and said she never wanted to go to a menagerie ever again.

The tiger had ripped the bottom of Pippi's dress. Pippi looked at the ragged material and said:

'Anyone got any scissors?'

Fräulein Paula had some, and she wasn't angry with Pippi any longer.

'Here you are, brave little girl,' she said, and handed

PIPPI AND MARKET DAY

Pippi the scissors. Pippi trimmed the dress way above her knees.

'There we are,' she said happily. 'Now I look even finer. Low cut at the top and the bottom. Anything twice as fine you'll never see.'

She strutted so elegantly that her knees knocked together for every step she took.

'Delightful,' she said as she walked along.

You might think things would calm down at the market after that, but markets are never really calm and it became perfectly clear that people had been too quick to breathe a sigh of relief.

In the tiny little town there was a troublemaker, an incredibly strong troublemaker. All the children were afraid of him. Even the police chose to step out of the way when Viggo the troublemaker was on the warpath. He wasn't angry all the time. Only when he had been drinking beer. And that is what he had been doing this market day. Roaring and bellowing, he came walking along Storgatan. He hit out on all sides with his terrible arms.

'Out of the way, you lice,' he bawled. 'Here comes Viggo!'

People flattened themselves against the walls of the buildings and many children wept in fear. There was no sign of the police. Eventually Viggo reached the place where the fairground was. He was a terrible sight to see, with his black hair hanging down over his forehead, his big red nose, and a yellow tooth sticking out of his mouth. The people down by the harbour thought he looked scarier than the tiger.

One little old man was selling sausages from a stall. Viggo walked up to him, thumped his fist on the counter and shouted:

'Give me a sausage and be quick about it!'

The old man instantly served him a sausage.

'That will be 25 öre,' he said, meekly.

'You want paying for the sausage, do you?' said Viggo. 'What, even when you're serving such a fine fellow as me! Know your place, old codger. Give me another one!'

The old man said he would like to be paid first for the sausage Viggo had already eaten. Then Viggo grabbed the man by his ears and shook him.

The old man didn't dare to disobey Viggo, but the people gathered all around couldn't help muttering angrily among themselves. One was even brave enough to say:

'Shame on you, treating an old man that way!'

Then Viggo turned around. He stared at the people with his bloodshot eyes.

'Did someone squeak?' he asked.

That made the people worried and they started to leave.

'Stand still!' roared Viggo. 'The first person to move will get the daylights knocked out of them. Stand still, I said! Because now Viggo is going to put on a little show.'

And he took a fistful of sausages and began juggling with them. He threw them into the air and caught some of them in his mouth and some with his hands, but he dropped a lot of them on the ground. The poor sausage-seller almost cried. Then a small figure broke away from the crowd.

Face to face with Viggo, Pippi came to a halt.

'Whose little lad can this be?' she said mildly. 'And what would his mother say if she saw him throwing his breakfast all over the place like this?'

Viggo let out a horrendous roar.

'Haven't I told you to stand still?' he bellowed.

'Do you always set your loudspeaker to the highest volume?' asked Pippi.

Viggo raised his fist and shouted: 'Brat! Must I beat you to a pulp before you learn to keep your mouth shut?'

Pippi stood with her hands at her sides and looked at him with interest.

'What was that you did with the sausages?' she asked. 'Was it this?'

And she flung Viggo high into the air and juggled him round and round for a while. Everyone cheered. The old sausage man clapped his wrinkly hands and smiled.

When Pippi had finished, an extremely petrified Viggo was left sitting on the ground, looking around in confusion.

'I think the town bully should go home now,' said Pippi.

Viggo had nothing against that.

'But first there are some sausages to be paid for,' said Pippi.

So Viggo stepped forward and paid for eighteen sausages. Then he left without a word. He was never the same again after that day.

'Long live Pippi!' shouted the people.

'Hurrah for Pippi!' said Tommy and Annika.

'We don't need the police in this town,' someone said. 'Not when we've got Pippi Longstocking.'

'That's for sure,' said another. 'She takes care of tigers and troublemakers both.'

'Of course you must have the police,' Pippi said. 'Someone has to make sure the bicycles are properly parked in the wrong place.'

'Oh, Pippi, how stylish you are,' said Annika, as the children wandered home from the market.

'Oh yes, delightful,' said Pippi. She hitched up her skirt that now only came down as far as her knees. 'Absolutely delightful, I must say.'

Chapter Six
Pippi is Shipwrecked

Every day, as soon as school was finished, Tommy and Annika raced over to Villa Villekulla. They didn't even want to do their homework at home, so they took their books with them to Pippi's.

'That's good,' said Pippi. 'Sit here and study then I'm sure a little knowledge will rub off on me. Not that it feels as if I need any, exactly, but perhaps to be a Fine Lady you need to know how many people live in Australia.'

Tommy and Annika sat at the kitchen table with their geography books open, and Pippi sat in the middle of the table with her legs crossed.

'Although, on the other hand,' said Pippi, laying a finger against her nose and thinking hard. 'What if I've just learned how many people live there and one of them goes and gets pneumonia and dies, then it will all have been a waste of time, and here I am, not like a Very Fine Lady at all.'

She thought again.

'Somebody should tell the people how to behave so there won't be any mistakes in your geography books,' she said.

When Tommy and Annika had finished their homework, the fun started. If the weather was good they played outside. They rode on the horse, clambered onto the roof of the mangle shed and sat there drinking coffee, or else they climbed up into the old oak tree that was completely hollow, so you could get down inside the trunk. Pippi said it was a most remarkable tree because it grew lemonade. The tree grew lemonade inside it. And that was probably true, because every time the children climbed down to their hiding place inside the oak tree, there stood three bottles of lemonade waiting for them. Tommy and Annika had no idea where the empty bottles went afterwards, but Pippi said they withered away as soon as they were empty. Yes, it really was a remarkable tree, Tommy and Annika both thought so. Sometimes chocolate bars grew there too, but only on Thursdays, said Pippi, so Tommy and Annika made sure to go there and pick chocolate bars every Thursday. Pippi said if you took time to water the tree properly in between, you could probably get it to grow bread rolls as well, and even a piece of roast beef.

If it was raining they stayed indoors, and that was far

PIPPI IS SHIPWRECKED

from boring. Either they could look at all the lovely things in Pippi's bureau drawers or they could sit in front of the fire and watch while Pippi made waffles or toasted apples, or else they could huddle inside the log box and listen as Pippi told them an exciting adventure story from the days she sailed the seas.

'Shiver me timbers, what a storm!' Pippi might say. 'Even the fish were seasick and wanted to go on dry land. And I saw a shark that was all green in the face and an octopus clutching its head with all its many arms. That storm was a corker!'

'Oh, Pippi, weren't you afraid?' asked Annika.

'Yes, what if you'd been shipwrecked?' said Tommy.

'Huh,' said Pippi. 'I've been more or less shipwrecked so many times I wasn't afraid at all, not me. At least, not to start with. I wasn't afraid when the prunes blew out of the custard when we were eating dinner, or even when the cook's false teeth flew out of his mouth. But when I saw that only the fur was left of the ship's cat, and the animal was whizzing off stark naked in a Far Easterly direction, well, then it started to feel a bit unpleasant.'

'I've got a book about a shipwreck,' said Tommy. '*Robinson Crusoe*, it's called.'

'Oh yes, that one's really good!' said Annika. 'And Robinson ended up on a desert island.'

'Pippi, have you ever been shipwrecked?' asked Tommy, sitting upright on the log box. 'And been washed ashore on a desert island?'

'I should jolly well say I have,' Pippi said, enthusiastically. 'Anyone more shipwrecked than me would be hard to find. Old Robinson's got nothing on me. I should imagine there are about eight or ten islands in the Atlantic and the Pacific where I *haven't* been washed ashore after a shipwreck. They're on a special blacklist in the tourist guidebooks.'

'Isn't it *fantastic* being on a desert island?' asked Tommy. 'It's something I'm longing to do myself.'

'It can be easily arranged,' said Pippi. 'There's no shortage of islands.'

'You're right. I know one not too far away,' said Tommy.

'Is it surrounded by water?' Pippi asked.

'Of course it is,' said Tommy.

'Good,' said Pippi. 'Because if it's on dry land it won't do.'

Tommy leaped around ecstatically.

'Let's do it!' he shouted. 'Let's do it right now!'

The school summer holidays were due to start in two days and at the same time Tommy and Annika's mum and dad would be going away. There couldn't be a better time for playing Robinson Crusoe.

'It's a good idea to have a boat first, if you're going to be shipwrecked,' said Pippi.

'And that's just what we haven't got,' said Annika.

'There's a broken old rowing boat on the river bed. I've seen it,' said Pippi.

'But that's already *been* shipwrecked,' said Annika.

'So much the better,' said Pippi. 'Now it knows what to do.'

It was a simple task for Pippi to rescue the sunken boat. She spent a whole day on the riverbank, waterproofing the hull with packing and pine tar, and spent one rainy morning in the woodshed chopping out a pair of oars.

Then it was Tommy and Annika's summer holidays and their parents went away.

'We'll be back in two days,' said the children's mother. 'I want you to be really good and obedient. And remember to do as Ella says.'

PIPPI IS SHIPWRECKED

Ella was the family's home help and she was going to be looking after Tommy and Annika while their parents were away. But as soon as the children were alone with Ella, Tommy said:

'You don't have to look after us, Ella, because we'll be with Pippi all the time.'

'And anyway, we can look after ourselves,' said Annika. 'Pippi *never* has anyone to look after her, so why can't we be left in peace for a measly two days?'

Ella had absolutely nothing against having a couple of days off, and after Tommy and Annika had nagged and pleaded and begged long enough, Ella said well, why not? She didn't mind travelling home to her mum for a spell. But in that case the children had to promise on their honour to eat and sleep properly and not run around outside in the evening without a warm jumper. Tommy said he'd be happy to wear twelve jumpers if only Ella would disappear.

So that's what happened. Ella disappeared and two hours later Pippi, Tommy and Annika, the horse, and Mr Nilsson set off on their journey to the desert island.

It was a mild, early-summer evening. The air was

warm even though the sky was overcast. It was quite a long way to the lake where the desert island lay. Pippi carried the boat upside down over her head, and she had loaded an enormous sack and a tent on the horse's back.

'What's in the sack?' asked Tommy.

'Food and guns and blankets and an empty bottle,' replied Pippi. 'Because I think we should have a more or less comfortable shipwreck, seeing as it's your first time. Otherwise when I'm shipwrecked I usually shoot an antelope or a llama and eat the flesh raw, but there *might* be a small chance that antelopes and llamas don't live on this island, and it would be so tiresome starving to death for such a minor reason.'

'What will you use the empty bottle for?' asked Annika.

'What will I use the empty bottle for? How can you ask such a stupid thing? A boat is the most important thing if you're going to be shipwrecked, of course, but an empty bottle comes next. My dad taught me that when I was still in my cradle. "Pippi," he said. "It doesn't matter if you forget to wash your feet when you are presented to the royal family, but if you forget to take

PIPPI IS SHIPWRECKED

an empty bottle with you when you're shipwrecked, you're done for."'

'Yes, but what do you *do* with it?' insisted Annika.

'Have you never heard of a message in a bottle?' said Pippi. 'You write a note asking for help and stuff it in the bottle, put in the cork and throw the bottle in the water. Then it floats straight off to someone who can come and rescue you. Blow me down, how else did you think people saved themselves after a shipwreck? Left it all to chance, eh? Oh no, no, no!'

'Oh, I see,' said Annika.

Soon they arrived at a small lake and there in the middle was the desert island. Just at that moment the sun burst through the clouds and cast a friendly shine over the fresh green bushes and trees.

'I do declare,' Pippi said, 'this is one of the nicest desert islands I have ever seen.'

She swiftly tipped the boat upright and slid it into the water. Then she took the load from the horse's back and stowed everything in the bottom of the boat. Annika and Tommy and Mr Nilsson jumped in. Pippi patted the horse.

PIPPI LONGSTOCKING GOES ABOARD

'Now, my dear horse, however much I want to, I can't ask you to sit in the boat. I hope you can swim. It's as easy as pie. All you do is this.'

She nosedived into the lake with her clothes on and swam about.

'It's ever so much fun, no kidding! And if you want to have more fun you can pretend to be a whale. Like this!'

Pippi filled her mouth with water, lay on her back and spouted out water like a fountain. The horse didn't think it was much fun, by the look of him, but when Pippi clambered back into the boat, picked up the oars and rowed off, he threw himself into the water and swam after them. But he didn't pretend to be a whale. When they were almost at the island Pippi yelled:

'All hands on deck!'

And a second later: 'Too late! We must abandon ship! Every man for himself!'

She stood in the stern and then plunged headfirst into the water. She soon surfaced, grabbed the boat's rope and swam towards land.

'I've got to save the food supplies anyway, so the crew might as well stay onboard,' she said. She tied the boat to a rock and helped Tommy and Annika ashore. Mr Nilsson could do it on his own.

'It's a miracle!' shouted Pippi. 'We've been saved. For now, at least. As long as there are no cannibals and lions here.'

By now the horse had reached the island. He trotted out of the water and gave himself a shake.

PIPPI IS SHIPWRECKED

'Look, here comes the first mate,' Pippi said happily. 'Let's decide on a plan of action.'

From the sack she took out a pistol that she had found once in a seaman's chest in the attic at Villa Villekulla. Waving the pistol in the air she stalked about, looking in all directions.

'What is it, Pippi?' Annika asked, anxiously.

'I thought I heard the snarl of a cannibal,' Pippi said. 'You can never be too careful. It would be just typical if I'd saved you from drowning only to see you served up alongside boiled vegetables as a cannibal's dinner.'

But there were no cannibals to be seen.

'Aha, they've hidden themselves and are waiting to pounce,' Pippi said. 'Or else they're sitting somewhere, looking through a recipe book and trying to work out how to cook us. I'll tell you something, if they serve me alongside boiled carrots I will never forgive them. I hate carrots.'

'Oh, Pippi, don't talk like that,' said Annika, and shuddered.

'What, don't you like carrots either? Not to worry, time to put the tent up.'

And that's what Pippi did. Soon it was put up in a sheltered place and Tommy and Annika crawled in and out again and were simply overjoyed. Just outside the tent Pippi lay some stones in a circle and gathered twigs and sticks to pile on top of it.

'Oh, how lovely, are we going to have a fire?' said Annika.

'We certainly are,' said Pippi. She took two pieces of wood and began rubbing them together. That made Tommy very interested.

'Gosh, Pippi,' he said. 'Are you going to make fire like the natives do?'

'No, but my hands are cold and this is one way of keeping them warm,' Pippi said. 'Now let me see, where did I put those matches?'

Soon a fire was burning brightly and Tommy said he thought it was very cosy.

'Yep, and it also keeps the wild beasts away,' said Pippi.

Annika gasped.

'What wild beasts?' she asked, her voice trembling.

'Mosquitoes,' said Pippi, distractedly scratching a large bite on her leg.

PIPPI IS SHIPWRECKED

Annika breathed a sigh of relief.

'And lions too, of course,' Pippi added. 'But it doesn't help against pythons or bison.' She patted her pistol. 'But keep calm, Annika,' she said. 'This'll save our skins, even if a little shrew does come along.'

Then Pippi served up sandwiches and coffee and the children sat around the fire and ate and drank and enjoyed themselves very much. Mr Nilsson sat on Pippi's shoulder and he ate as well, and the horse stuck his nose in from time to time and was given a piece of bread and some sugar. He had lots and lots of tasty green grass to eat as well.

The sky was cloudy and darkness fell among the bushes. Annika moved as close to Pippi as she could get. The flames cast such strange shadows. It felt as if the darkness was alive outside their little circle that was lit up by the fire. Annika shivered. What if a cannibal was standing behind that tall juniper bush? Or a lion hiding behind that big rock?

Pippi put down her coffee mug.

'Fifteen men on a dead man's chest, Yo ho ho and a bottle of rum!'

she sang in a croaky voice.

Annika shivered even more.

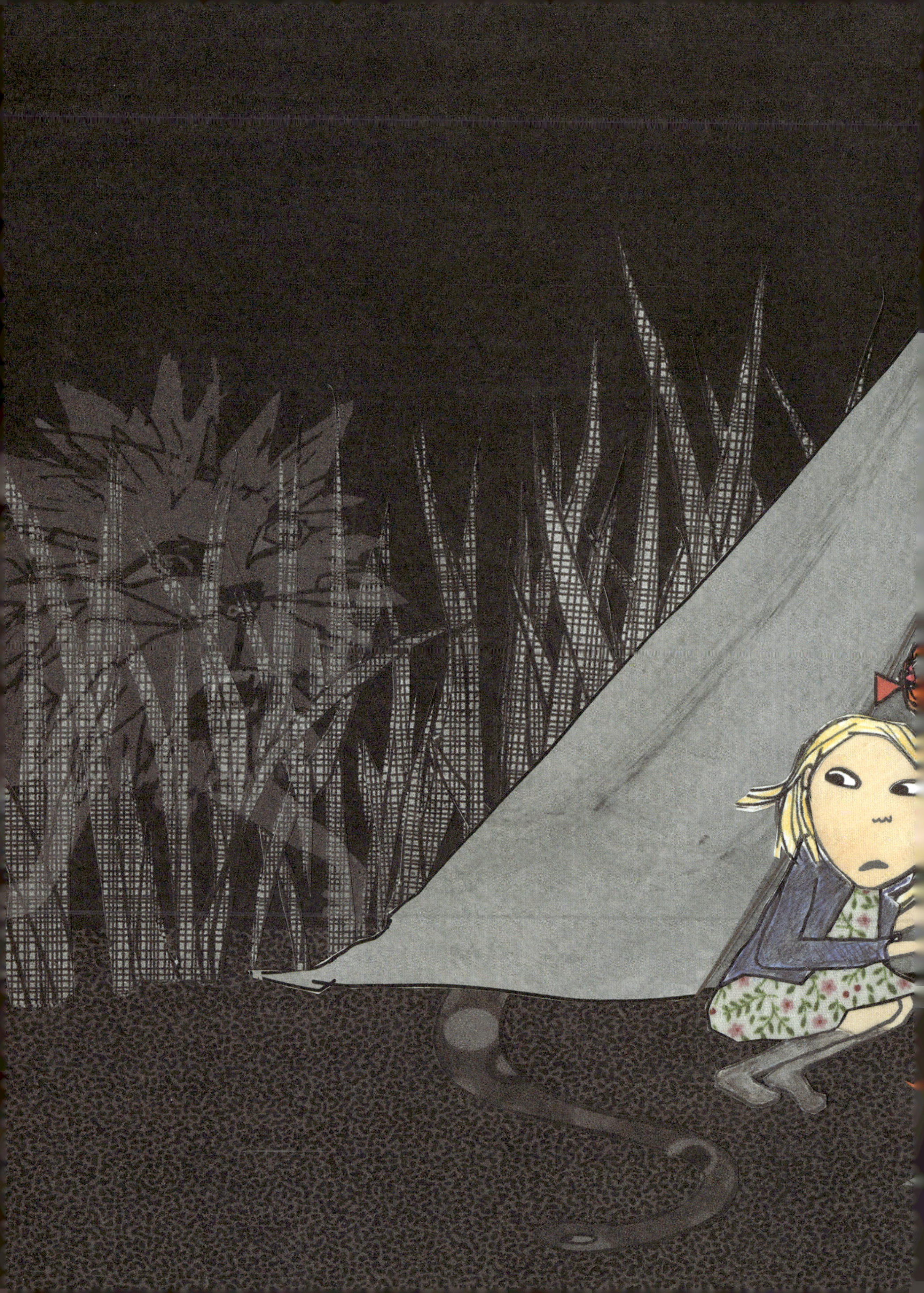

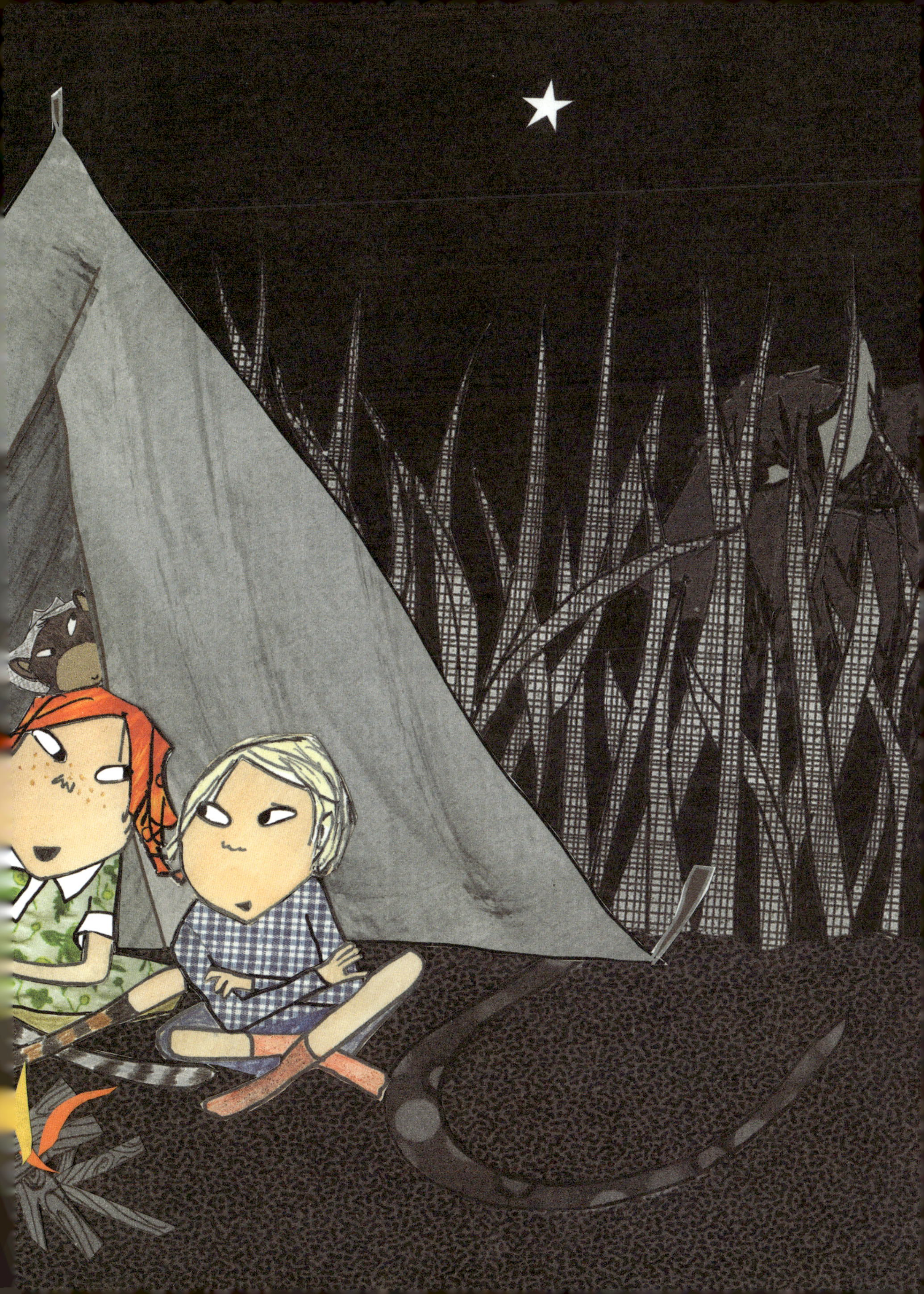

'That song is in a book I've got at home,' Tommy said, excitedly. 'A book about pirates.'

'You don't say?' said Pippi. 'Then I expect Fridolf wrote that book, because he's the one who taught it to me. Who knows how many times I've sat in the stern of my dad's boat on a starry night, with the Southern Cross overhead and Fridolf beside me singing:

"Fifteen men on a dead man's chest,

Yo ho ho and a bottle of rum!"'

Pippi sang again and her voice was even croakier than before.

'Pippi, I get such a funny feeling inside when you sing like that,' said Tommy. 'It feels scary but brilliant at the same time.'

'Inside me it's mostly scary,' said Annika. 'But a tiny bit brilliant too.'

'I'm going to sea when I grow up,' Tommy stated. 'I'm going to be a pirate. Just like you, Pippi.'

'Terrific,' said Pippi. 'The Dread of the Caribbean Sea, that's what we'll be, you and me, Tommy. We'll plunder gold and jewels and hide our treasure inside a cave on a desert island in the Pacific Ocean, and three skellingtons will stand guard, and we'll have a flag with a skull and crossbones on it and we'll sing "Yo Ho Ho" so loud it will be heard from one side of the Atlantic to the other, and all the seafarers will turn as white as a sheet when they hear us and want to throw themselves overboard rather than face our bloodthirsty revenge!'

'But what about me?' moaned Annika. 'I'm too scared to be a pirate. What can I do?'

'Oh, you can come anyway,' Pippi said. 'And dust the piano!'

Slowly the fire died down.

'Off to our bunks,' said Pippi. She had spread fir tree branches on the ground inside the tent, and on top of that a thick layer of blankets.

'Do you want to sleep head to toe with me in the tent?' Pippi asked the horse. 'Or would you rather stand here under a tree with a horse blanket? Sleeping in a tent makes you feel sick, did you say? Well, as you please!' And Pippi gave him a friendly pat.

Soon all three children and Mr Nilsson lay rolled up in blankets inside the tent. Outside the waves lapped the shore.

'Hear the sighing of the ocean waves,' said Pippi, sleepily.

It was as dark as a coal mine and Annika held Pippi's hand because things felt much less dangerous that way. All at once it started to rain. The drops pattered on the tent but inside it was warm and dry, which made it nice to hear the pattering. Pippi went out and put another blanket over the horse. He stood under a thick tree, so he was perfectly fine.

'Oh, how snug we are in here,' sighed Tommy, when Pippi came back.

'You can say that again,' said Pippi. 'And look what I found under a rock! Three bars of chocolate!'

Three minutes later Annika was fast asleep with her mouth full of chocolate and Pippi's hand in hers.

'We forgot to clean our teeth,' said Tommy, and then he fell asleep as well.

When Tommy and Annika woke up, Pippi had disappeared. They scrambled out of the tent. The sun was shining. In front of the tent a new fire was burning and Pippi was sitting by the flames, frying bacon and boiling coffee.

'Greetings, my hearties, and Happy Easter,' she said, when she saw Tommy and Annika.

'Twerp, it's not Easter,' said Tommy.

'Fancy that,' said Pippi. 'Save it for next year, then!'

The marvellous smell of bacon and coffee filled the children's noses. They sat cross-legged round the fire and Pippi passed them fried bacon and eggs and potatoes. Afterwards they drank coffee with ginger biscuits. Never had a breakfast tasted so wonderful.

'I think we're much better off than Robinson Crusoe,' said Tommy.

'Yes, and if we can catch some fresh fish for dinner then I'm afraid Robinson will turn blue with envy,' said Pippi.

'Yuk, I don't like fish,' said Tommy.

'Neither do I,' said Annika.

But Pippi cut a long, thin twig, tied a piece of string to it, made a hook out of a safety pin, attached a scrap of bread to the hook and sat herself down on a large rock beside the water.

'Hmm, let's see,' she said.

'What are you trying to catch?' asked Tommy.

'Squid,' said Pippi. 'Nothing compares to it!'

She sat there for a whole hour, but no squid took the bait. A pike came up and sniffed the bread, but Pippi jerked the hook out of the water.

'No thanks, matey,' she said. 'Looks like it'll be pancakes for us today. The squid are playing hard to get.'

Tommy and Annika were very happy. The water glittered invitingly in the sunshine.

'Let's go swimming,' said Tommy.

Pippi and Annika agreed. The water was pretty cold. Tommy and Annika both dipped in a big toe but quickly drew it out again.

'I know a better way,' said Pippi. There was a rock right on the water's edge and on top of the rock was a tree. Its branches stretched out over the water. Pippi climbed up the tree and tied a rope around a branch.

'Watch this,' she said, and she grabbed the rope, threw herself into the air and plummeted into the water.

'In straight away, no dithering,' she called, as she came to the surface.

Tommy and Annika were doubtful at first, but it

PIPPI IS SHIPWRECKED

looked such fun they decided to give it a try. And once they had tried, they never wanted to stop, because it was even more fun than it looked. Mr Nilsson wanted to join in. He slid down the rope but a split second before he hit the water he whirled round and shot up the rope again. He did that every time, even though the children yelled at him and called him a coward. Then Pippi discovered you could sit on an old plank and toboggan down the rock into the lake, and that was fun too because it made an almighty splash when they smacked into the water.

'That Robinson fellow, do you reckon he tobogganed on a plank?' Pippi asked, as she sat on the top of the rock, ready go again.

'Hardly likely,' said Tommy. 'It doesn't say so in the book, anyway.'

'Just as I thought. His shipwreck wasn't up to much. What did he do all day? A nice bit of embroidery? Yippee, here I go!'

Pippi glided down the rock with her red plaits flapping around her.

After their swim the children decided to explore the island properly.

All three sat on the horse

and he trotted off obediently.

Uphill and down they went,

through tangled bushes

and crowded pine trees,

over bogs and across pretty open

glades full of meadow flowers.

Pippi sat with her pistol at the ready, and now and then she fired a shot that made the horse leap into the air in fright.

'That's one less lion,' she said, pleased with herself.

Either that or:

'Now *that* cannibal has eaten his last meat pie!'

'I think this island should be ours for ever,' said Tommy, when they returned to their camp and Pippi had started making pancakes and ham.

Pippi and Annika agreed.

The pancakes were delicious when they were served scorching hot. There were no plates and no knives or forks to be seen, so Annika asked:

'Can we eat with our fingers?'

'Fine by me,' Pippi said. 'But I'll do it the old-fashioned way and eat with my mouth.'

'Oh, you know what I mean,' Annika said. She picked up a pancake in her small hand and crammed it blissfully into her mouth.

Then it was evening again. The fire was out. Close together and with their faces smeared with pancake, the children lay in their blankets. A large star was shining down through a crack in the tent. The sighing of the waves lulled them to sleep.

PIPPI IS SHIPWRECKED

'We've got to go home today,' Tommy grumbled next morning.

'That's too bad,' said Annika. 'I want to be here all summer. But Mum and Dad are coming home today.'

After breakfast Tommy went for a stroll along the shore. All of a sudden he gave a cry. The boat! It had vanished! Annika was frantic. How would they get off the island? She might have wanted to stay on the island all summer, but it was quite a different thing to know you *couldn't* get home! And what would their poor mother say when she realized Tommy and Annika were gone! Annika's eyes filled with tears at the very thought.

'Cheer up, Annika,' said Pippi. 'What exactly did you think a shipwreck was? And what do you think Robinson would have said if a ship had come sailing past after he'd been on that island for two days? "After you, Mr Crusoe. Hop aboard and be saved and take a nice bath and have your toenails trimmed!" I think old Crusoe would have run and hid in the bushes. Because once you've come to a desert island you want to be there for leastwise seven years.'

Seven years! Annika shuddered and Tommy looked very thoughtful.

'No, I don't mean we'll be here for ever,' Pippi said, reassuringly. 'When Tommy has to do his military service, then we'll let people know we're here, I suppose,' she said.

That made Annika even more distressed. Pippi looked at her for a while.

'Oh well, if you feel like that about it,' she said, 'There's nothing for it but to send a message in a bottle.'

PIPPI IS SHIPWRECKED

She walked over and pulled the bottle out of the sack. She managed to find a pen and paper too. She laid it all out on a rock in front of Tommy.

'You can do the writing bit, you're more used to it,' she said.

'All right, but what shall I write?' said Tommy.

'Let me think,' said Pippi.

'You can write this:

"HELP US BEFORE WE PERISH! On this island without snuff for two days and fading FAST."

'We can't say that, Pippi,' Tommy said. 'It isn't true.'

'What isn't?' asked Pippi.

'We can't write "without snuff",' said Tommy.

'Can't we?' said Pippi. 'Have you got any snuff?'

'No,' said Tommy.

'Has Annika got any snuff?'

'Of course not, but . . .'

'Have I got any snuff?'

'That might be true,' Tommy said. 'But we don't use snuff, do we?'

'That's exactly what I want you to write. "Without snuff for two days . . ."'

'But if you write that, I'm sure people will think we *use* snuff,' Tommy insisted.

'All right, Tommy,' said Pippi. 'Answer me this! Which people are most often without snuff, the ones who use it or the ones who *don't*?'

'The ones who *don't*, of course,' said Tommy.

'Well then, what are you arguing about?' said Pippi. 'Write what I said!'

So Tommy wrote:

'Help us before we perish! On this island without

snuff for two days and fading away fast.'

Pippi took the piece of paper, pushed it into the bottle, put in a cork and threw the bottle into the water.

'Our rescuers will soon be here,' she said.

The bottle bobbed away and soon settled nicely between some roots on the shore.

'We've got to throw it further out,' said Tommy.

'That would be the stupidest thing to do,' said Pippi. 'Because if the bottle floats far away, our rescuers won't know where to find us. But if it stays here, we can call to them when they find it and we'll be saved in a flash.'

Pippi sat down by the water.

'Best to keep an eye on that bottle at all times,' she said. Tommy and Annika sat down beside her. After ten minutes Pippi said impatiently:

'People must think we've got nothing better to do than wait to be rescued. Where can they have got to?'

'Who?' asked Annika.

'Our rescuers,' said Pippi. 'It shows an utterly disgraceful lack of concern, when you consider that human lives are at stake.'

Annika began to think they really would fade away on the island. But suddenly Pippi stuck a finger in the air and yelled:

'Bless my soul, how absent-minded I am! How *could* I have forgotten!'

'Forgotten what?' asked Tommy.

'The boat,' said Pippi. 'I carried it up on dry land last night, of course, after you'd gone to sleep!'

'What did you do that for?' Annika reprimanded her.

'I was afraid it would get wet,' said Pippi. Like a shot she fetched the boat, which was well hidden under a fir tree. She hurled it into the water and said grimly:

'There, let them come now! And when they *do* come to save us it will be a waste of time because we're going to save ourselves. Serve them right! They'll have to learn to get a move on next time.'

'I hope we get home before Mum and Dad,' said Annika, as they sat in the boat and Pippi rowed energetically towards land. 'Oh, how worried they will be otherwise!'

'I don't think so,' said Pippi.

But Mr and Mrs Settergren got home a full half hour before the children. There was no sign of Tommy and

PIPPI IS SHIPWRECKED

Annika, but in the letterbox was a sheet of paper with the words:

DON'T GO THINKING YOR KIDS ARR ded OR MISSin cos THAY seRTiNLY ARR NOT JUST A BIT SHiPPReKkED BUT THAY WILL BEE HOME SOON I SWARE YORS SINSEERLEE PiPPi

Chapter Seven

Pippi Has a Special Visitor

One summer evening Pippi, Tommy, and Annika were sitting on Pippi's veranda eating the wild strawberries they had picked that morning. It was such a lovely evening, what with the birdsong and the scent of flowers, and the wild strawberries too, of course. It was very peaceful. The children ate and hardly said a word. Tommy and Annika were thinking how wonderful it was now summer was here, and how good it was that school wouldn't be starting for ages. What Pippi was thinking wasn't easy to guess.

'Pippi, you've been living in Villa Villekulla a whole year now,' said Annika unexpectedly, and she squeezed Pippi's arm.

'Yes, time flies and I'm starting to get old,' said Pippi. 'When autumn comes I'll be ten, and my best years will be behind me.'

'Do you think you'll live here for ever?' asked Tommy. 'I mean, until you're big enough to be a pirate?'

'Who knows,' said Pippi. 'I don't think my dad will be staying on that island forever. As soon as he gets a new boat I expect he'll come and fetch me.'

Tommy and Annika sighed. Suddenly Pippi sat bolt upright on the veranda step.

'Oh look, here he comes, by the way,' she said, pointing towards the gate. She was down the garden path in three hops. Tommy and Annika followed her shyly, but fast enough to see her throw her arms around a considerably plump individual with a stubbly moustache and blue sailor trousers.

'Daddy Ephraim!' yelled Pippi, and she kicked her legs so wildly as she clung around his neck that her long shoes fell off. 'Daddy Ephraim, how you've grown!'

'Pippilotta Victoriaria Tea-cosy Appleminta Ephraim's-daughter Longstocking, my beloved child! I was about to say how YOU have grown!'

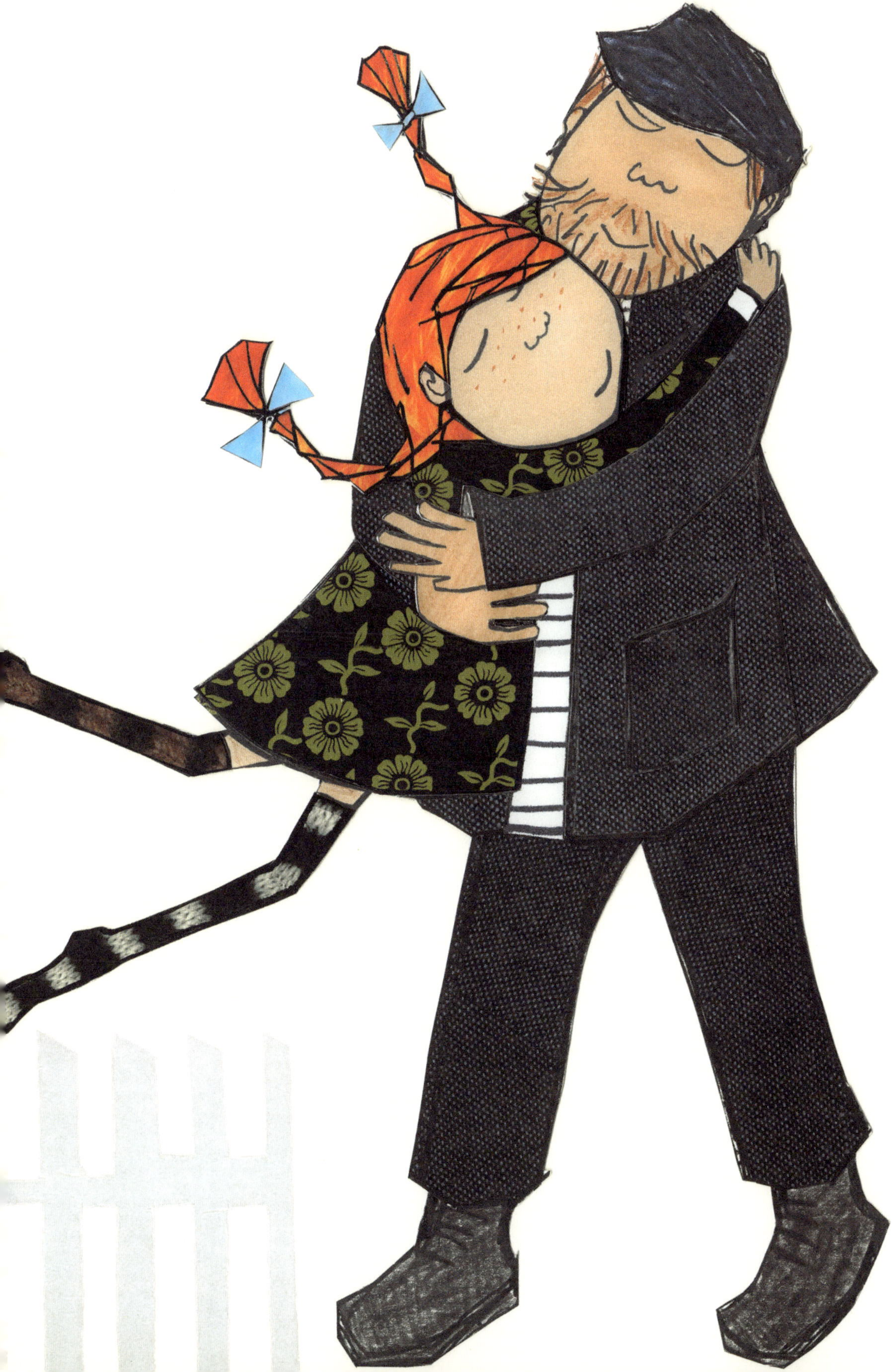

'I know,' said Pippi. 'That's why I said it first.'

'Are you as strong as you used to be, my child?'

'Stronger,' said Pippi. 'Want to arm-wrestle?'

'What are we waiting for?' said Daddy Ephraim.

There was a table in the garden and Pippi and her father sat down at it, ready to start arm-wrestling, while Tommy and Annika looked on. There was only one person in the whole wide world stronger than Pippi, and that was her father. There they sat, trying as hard as they could, but neither of them managed to beat the other. Eventually Daddy Ephraim's arm began to tremble ever so slightly and Pippi said:

'When I'm ten, I'll beat you, Daddy Ephraim.'

Pippi's dad agreed.

'Goodness gracious,' said Pippi. 'I forgot to do the introductions. This is Tommy and Annika, and this is my dad, Captain His Majesty Ephraim Longstocking—you are a king, aren't you, Dad?'

'That I am,' said Captain Longstocking. 'I am King of all the Koratutts, on the island of Koratuttutt. I floated ashore after I blew overboard, as you recall.'

'I guessed something like that had happened,' said

Pippi. 'I knew all along you hadn't drowned.'

'Me, drowned? Oh no! It's as impossible for me to drown as it is for a camel to thread a needle. My blubber keeps me afloat.'

Tommy and Annika looked at Captain Longstocking in wonder.

'Why aren't you wearing any Koratutt clothes?' Tommy asked.

'They're in my rucksack,' said Captain Longstocking.

'Put them on, put them on!' shouted Pippi. 'I want to see my dad in his royal finery.'

So they all went into the kitchen. Captain Longstocking disappeared into Pippi's room, and the children sat on the log box and waited.

'It's just like being at the theatre,' said Annika, excitedly.

And then—

CRASH –

the door flew open and there stood the King of the Koratutts. He had a grass skirt around his waist, a gold crown on his head and long rows of beads round his neck. In one hand he carried a spear and in the other a shield. And that was about all, apart from the golden ankle bracelets decorating a pair of thick hairy legs poking out from under the grass skirt.

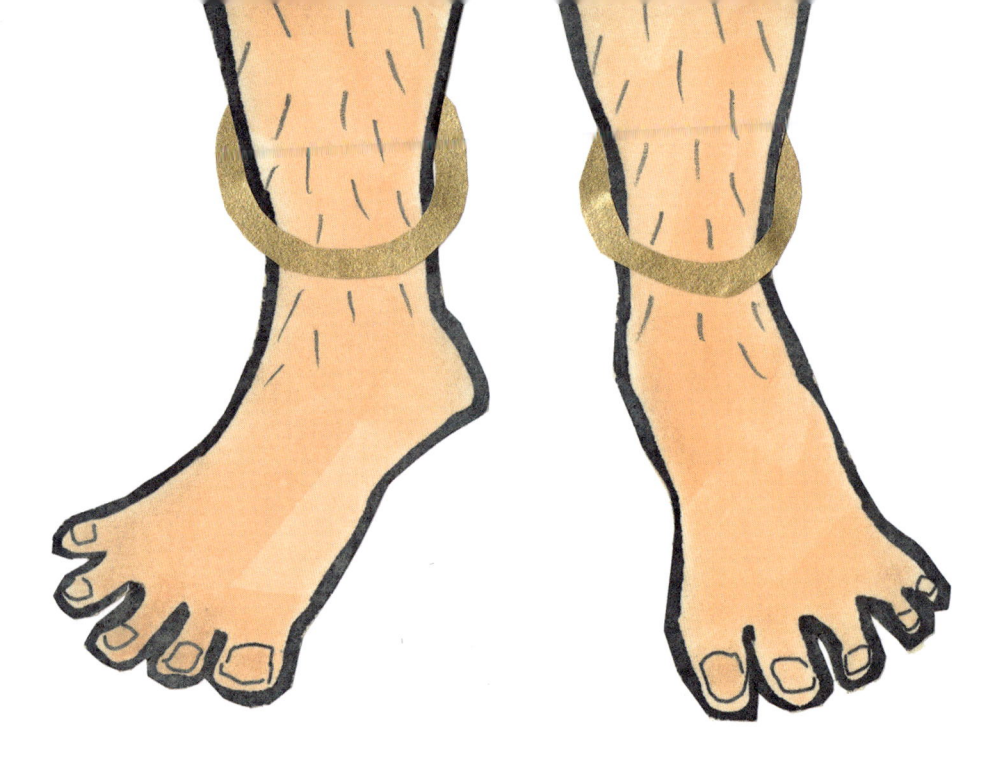

'**Ussamkussor mussor filibussor**,' said Captain Longstocking, frowning threateningly.

'Crikey,' Tommy said, thrilled. 'What does that mean, Mr Ephraim, sir?'

'It means: "Tremble, my enemies!"'

'But, Daddy Ephraim,' said Pippi, 'weren't the Koratutts surprised when you washed up on their island?'

'That they were, very surprised indeed,' said Captain Longstocking. 'But when they saw me pull up a palm tree by the roots with my bare hands they made me king. Then I ruled over them every morning and worked on my boat every afternoon. It took a long time to build it when I had to do it all on my own. It was only a little sailing boat, of course. When it was ready I told the Koratutts that I would be going away for a while but I would soon be back and I would have a princess called Pippilotta with me. And they thumped their shields and hollered: "**Ussumplussor, ussumplussor!**"'

'What does that mean?' asked Annika.

'It means: "Bravo, bravo!" I ruled over them frantically for fourteen days, so it would be enough to last all the time I was away. Then I hoisted the sail and set off out to sea, and all the Koratutts shouted: "**Ussumkura kussomkara!**" And that meant: "Welcome back again, fat white chieftain!" Then I set course straight for Surabaya. And what do you think was the first thing I espied when I jumped ashore? Nothing other than my faithful old ship, the *Hoppetossa*. And my faithful old Fridolf, leaning on the railing and waving madly. "Fridolf, old bucko," I said, "I'm taking over command of the ship." "Aye aye, cap'n," he said. And that's what I did.

The old crew was still aboard and now the *Hoppetossa* is moored in the harbour, so you can go and say hello to all your old friends, Pippi.'

That made Pippi so happy she stood on her head on the kitchen table and waggled her legs. But Tommy and Annika couldn't help feeling a little sad. It was

PIPPI HAS A SPECIAL VISITOR

exactly as if someone was taking Pippi away from them, they thought.

'Time for a celebration!' shouted Pippi, when she was back on her feet again. 'We'll celebrate until Villa Villekulla's roof flies off!'

Then she covered the kitchen table with piles of food and everyone sat down and ate. Pippi gobbled down three hard-boiled eggs, shell and all. From time to time she bit her dad's ear, just because she was so pleased to see him. Mr Nilsson, who had been sleeping, bounded up and rubbed his eyes in astonishment when he saw Captain Longstocking.

'Shiver me timbers, you haven't still got Mr Nilsson?' said Captain Longstocking.

'Yes indeedy, and I've got another pet, believe it or not,' Pippi said, and she went and fetched the horse. He was given a hard-boiled egg to nibble, too.

Captain Longstocking was very pleased that Pippi had made everything so nice for herself in Villa Villekulla, and he was delighted that she'd had her travel bag full of golden coins, which meant she hadn't gone without anything while he was away.

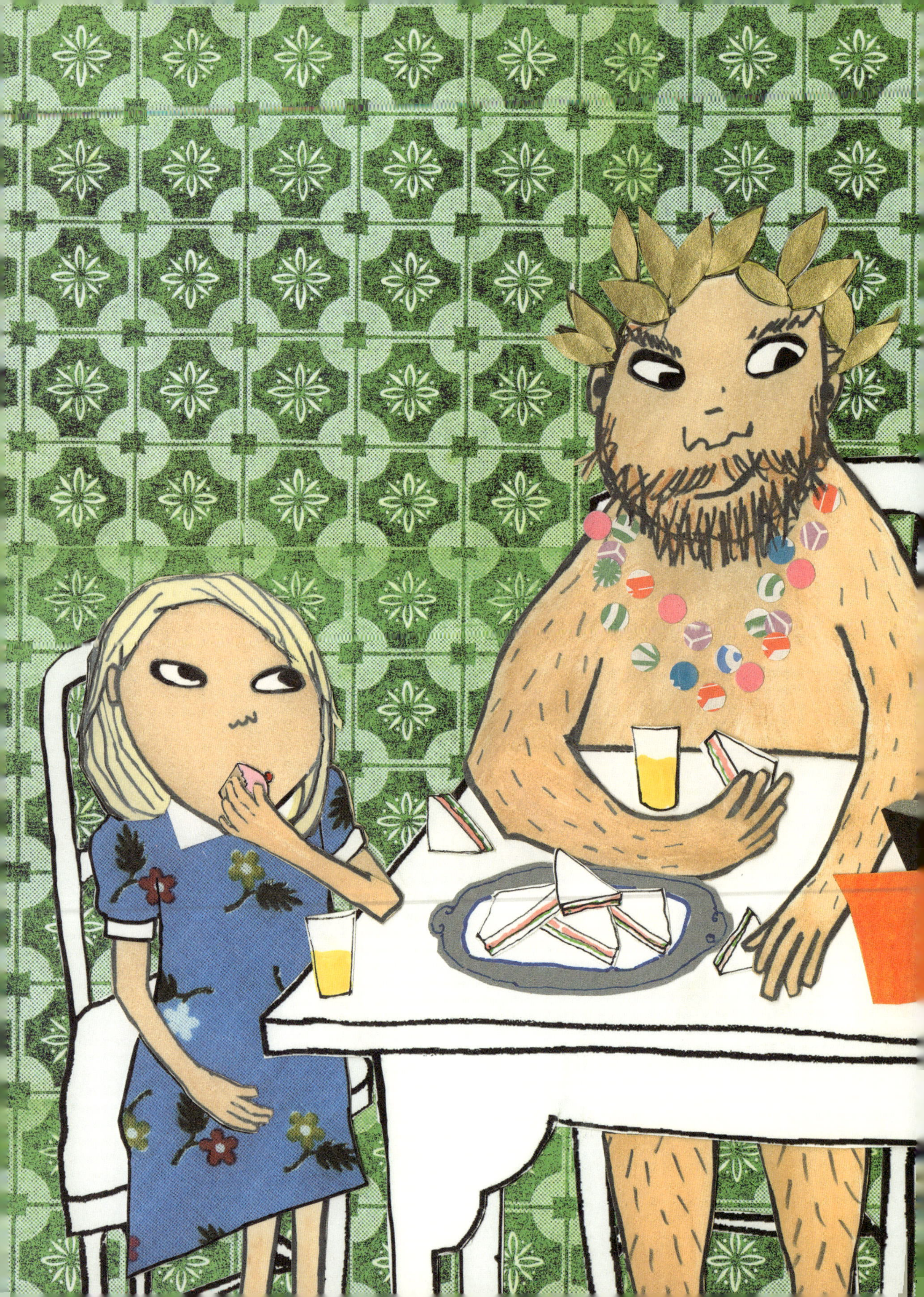

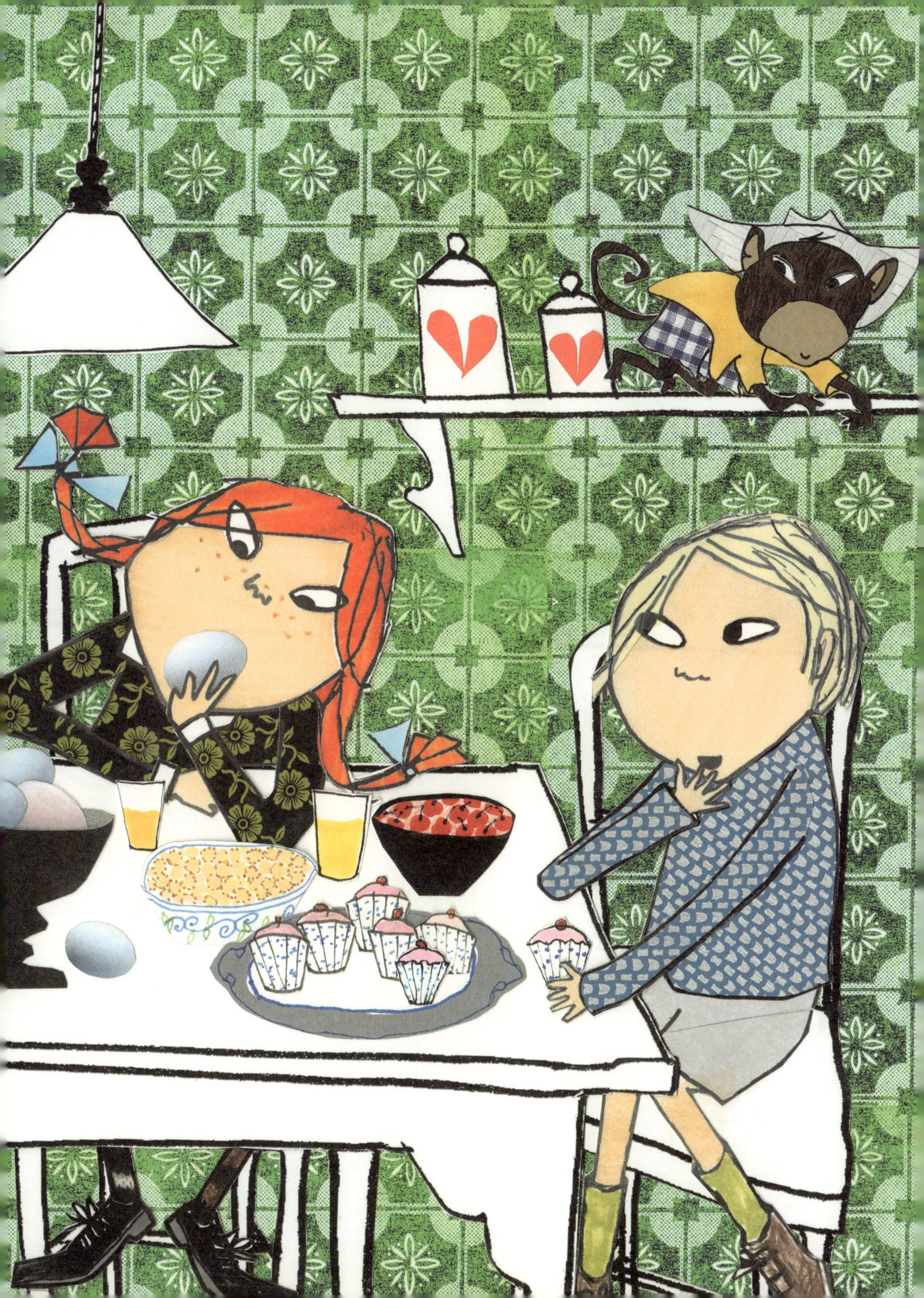

When everyone had eaten themselves full, Captain Longstocking pulled a ceremonial drum from his rucksack, the kind the Koratutts used to beat when they had their dances and rituals. And Captain Longstocking sat on the floor and drummed on the drum. It sounded muffled and strange, unlike anything Tommy and Annika had heard before.

Pippi took off her big shoes and danced in her stockings, and that dance was also strange.

Finally, Captain Longstocking did a wild war dance he had learned on Koratuttutt island. He swung his spear and waved his shield about, and his naked feet thumped so hard Pippi had to shout: 'Mind you don't go through the kitchen floor!'

'That doesn't matter,' said Captain Longstocking, and whirled even faster. 'Because now you're going to be a Koratutt princess, my precious daughter!'

Pippi jumped up and began dancing with her father. They whirled round together, cheering and shouting, and occasionally made terrific leaps into the air.

It made Tommy and Annika dizzy to watch them.

Clearly Mr Nilsson felt the same because he sat with his hands over his eyes the whole time.

After a while the dance turned into a wrestling match between Pippi and her father. Captain Longstocking hurled his daughter through the air and she landed on the hat rack. But she wasn't there for long. With a yell she made a gigantic leap right across the kitchen, aiming straight for her father. A second later she slung him round and he flew like a meteor head first into the log box, with his fat legs sticking out. He couldn't get himself out, partly because he was too fat and partly because he was laughing so heartily. A rumbling like thunder came from the log box. Pippi grabbed hold of his feet to pull him out, but that made him laugh so much he almost suffocated. Captain Longstocking was a particularly ticklish man.

'Stop ti-i-i-ckling me!' he gasped. **'Throw me in the sea or chuck me out of the window, whatever you want, but don't tickle my feet!'**

He laughed so much that Tommy and Annika were afraid the log box would burst. Eventually he managed to wriggle his way out of the box, and as soon as he was on his feet he rushed at Pippi and flung her helplessly across the kitchen.

Pippi let out a yell and threw herself at her father.

She gave him such a battering that the grass skirt tore and dried grass filled the kitchen. His gold crown fell off and rolled under the table. Finally Pippi managed to bring her dad to the floor. She sat on him and said:

'**Admit you are defeated!**'

'**Yes, I'm defeated,**' said Captain Longstocking, and they laughed and laughed. Pippi gave her dad's nose a playful nip and he said:

'I haven't had this much fun since you and I threw everyone out of the seamen's tavern in Singapore!'

He crawled under the table to get his crown.

'Lucky the Koratutts can't see this,' he said. 'The royal regalia, lying under the kitchen table at Villa Villekulla.'

He sat the crown on his head and straightened out the grass skirt, which was looking quite straggly and thin.

'Looks like it needs stuffing,' said Pippi.

'Yes, but it was worth it,' said Captain Longstocking.

He sat on the floor and wiped the sweat from his forehead.

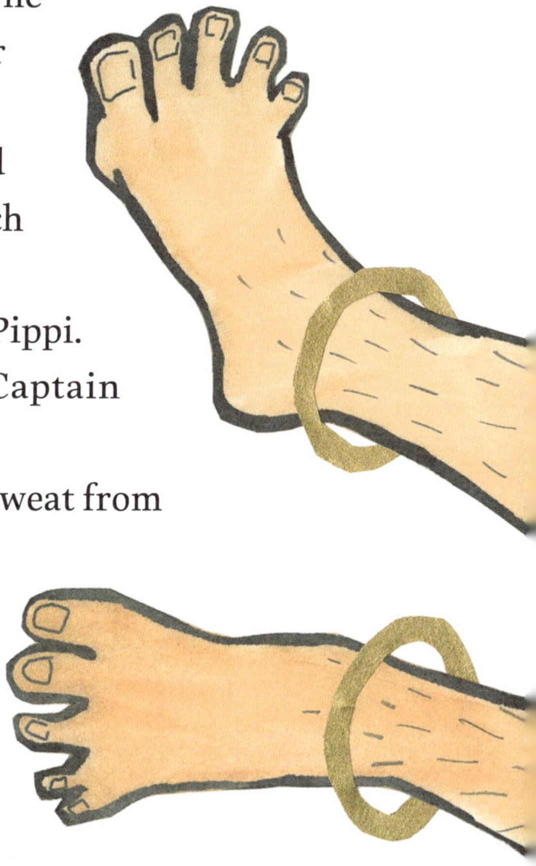

'Now, Pippi, my child,' he said. 'Are you doing much lying these days?'

'Oh yes, when I get the time, which isn't very often,' Pippi replied, modestly. 'What about you? You weren't so bad at lying yourself, if I remember rightly.'

'Oh, I usually lie a little to the Koratutts on a Saturday evening, if they have behaved themselves during the week. We usually have a song and lying evening with drum accompaniment and a torchlit dance. The worse I lie, the louder they beat the drum.'

'Fancy that,' said Pippi. 'No one beats a drum for me, that's for sure. Here I am on my own, lying myself silly, but no one so much as blows a tin whistle because of it. The other evening, after I'd gone to bed, I made up a long story about a calf that could knit socks and climb trees, and guess what? I believed every single word! That's what I call excellent lying! But as for beating a drum—oh no, not a soul does that!'

'In that case, I will,' said Captain Longstocking. And he played a long drum roll for his daughter, and Pippi sat on his lap and leaned her face against his chin.

Annika had been standing there, thinking about

PIPPI HAS A SPECIAL VISITOR

something. She didn't know if it was the right thing to say, but she couldn't stop herself.

'It's bad to lie,' she said. 'That's what my mum says.'

'Oh, don't be such an idiot, Annika,' said Tommy. 'Pippi isn't really lying, she's pretending to lie. She's making it up, don't you see, you ninny?'

Pippi looked at Tommy seriously.

'Sometimes you say such sensible things I'm afraid something very good will come of you,' she said.

By now it was evening and time for Tommy and Annika to go home. It had been an eventful day and such fun to see a real live King of the Koratutts. And of course, it was nice for Pippi that her dad had come home. But still!

When Tommy and Annika were tucked up in their beds they didn't chat like they usually did. It was totally silent in the children's room. Suddenly there was a sigh. It was Tommy. And a moment later there was another sigh. This time it was Annika.

'What are you sighing for?' said Tommy, irritably.

But he didn't get an answer because Annika was lying with her head under the covers, weeping.

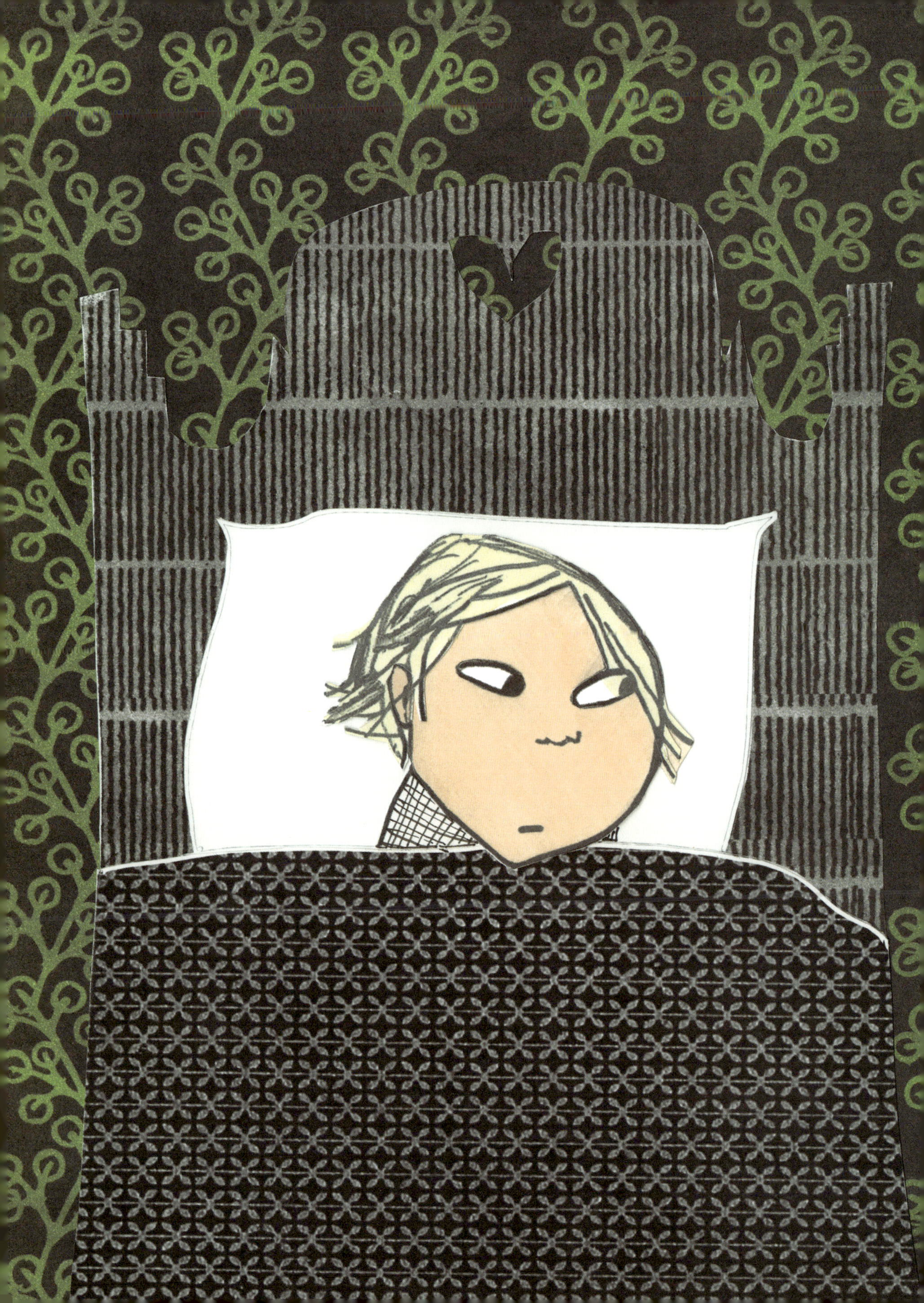

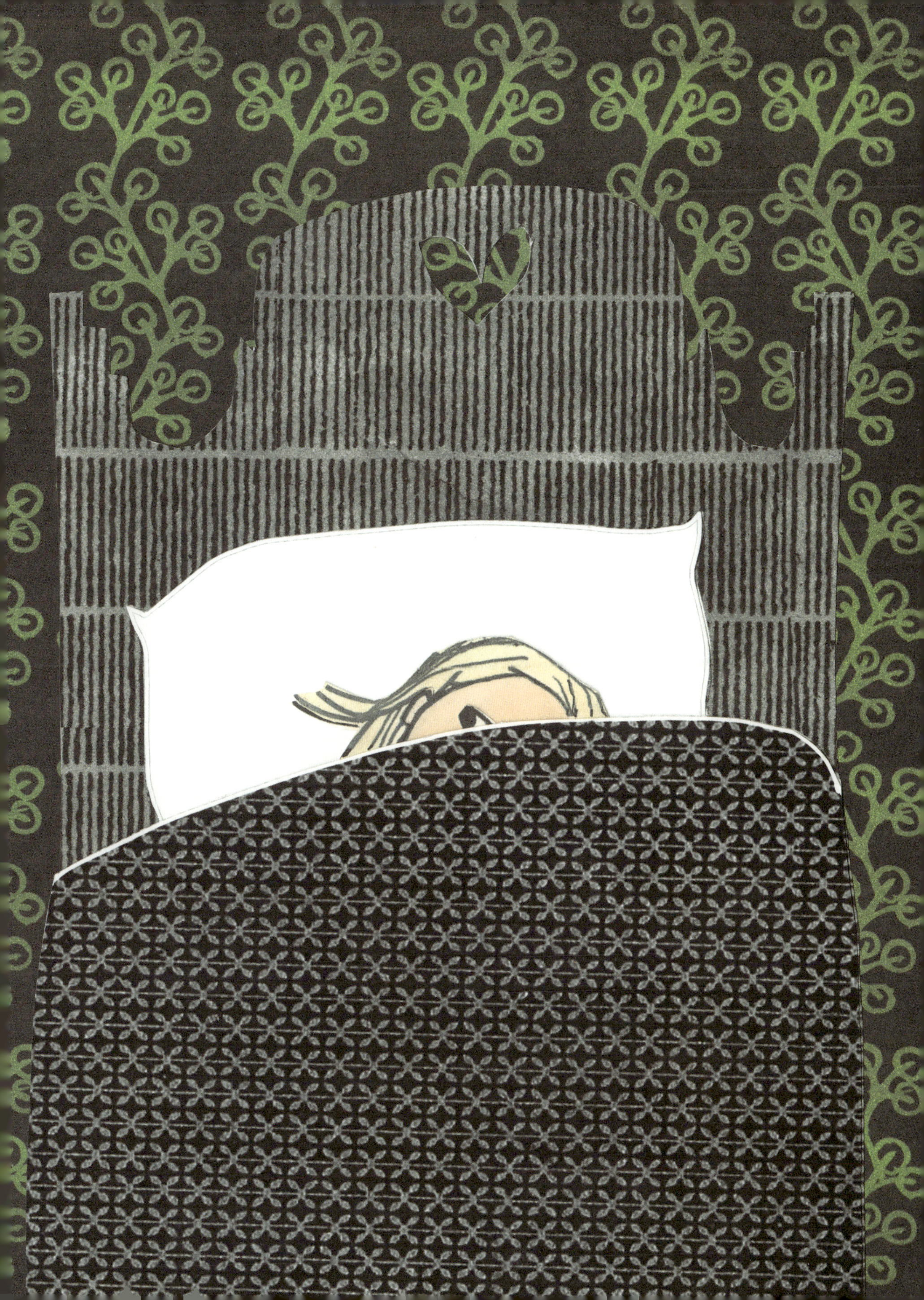

Chapter Eight

Pippi Has a Leaving Party

When Tommy and Annika walked through Villa Villekulla's kitchen door next morning, the whole house was echoing with the most horrendous snoring. Captain Longstocking hadn't woken up yet. But Pippi was there. She had been busy with her morning exercises in the middle of the kitchen floor when Tommy and Annika arrived and interrupted her.

'Well, that's my future settled,' she said. 'I'm going to be a Koratutt princess as well as sail the oceans of the world for six months aboard the *Hoppetossa*. Dad thinks if he rules the Koratutts properly for one half of the year, they'll be able to do without a king for the other half. Because you see, an old seadog needs to feel the deck under his feet now and again. And he has my upbringing to think about as well. If I'm going to be a first-rate pirate then living the life of royalty won't be enough. It turns you into a softy, Dad says.'

'Won't you be coming to Villa Villekulla at all?' asked Tommy in a low voice.

'Yep, when we retire,' said Pippi. 'In about fifty or sixty years' time, give or take. And then we'll play together and have a nice time.'

That wasn't much comfort for Tommy and Annika.

'Imagine that—a Koratutt princess,' Pippi said, lost in thought. 'Not many children get to become one of those. Oh, I'll be so grand! I'll have rings in all my ears and a slightly bigger one in my nose.' She sighed with delight. 'Princess Pippilotta! What a life! What splendour! And oh, how I'll dance! Princess Pippilotta, dancing in the firelight to the thundering drums. Just think how my nose rings will rattle!'

'When . . . when . . . are you leaving?' asked Tommy. His voice sounded faintly rusty.

'The *Hoppetossa* sets sail tomorrow,' said Pippi.

All three children stood in silence for a long while. There didn't seem to be any more to say. Finally, Pippi did one more somersault and said:

'But this very evening there will be a leaving party at Villa Villekulla. A leaving party, I'm not saying any more! Everyone who wants to come and say goodbye to me will be most welcome.'

The news spread like wildfire among the children in the tiny little town.

PIPPI HAS A LEAVING PARTY

'Pippi Longstocking is going away and she's having a leaving party this evening in Villa Villekulla. Anybody who wants to can go!'

There were many children who did want to go. Thirty-four, to be precise. Tommy and Annika's mum had promised to let them stay up as late as they liked that night. She understood it was an absolute necessity.

Tommy and Annika would never forget the evening Pippi had her leaving party. It was one of those phenomenally hot, beautiful summer evenings when you tell yourself:

'This is what summer is really like!'

All the roses in Pippi's garden shone in the twilight and perfumed the air. The old trees sighed secretively. Everything would have been so wonderful, if only. If only! Tommy and Annika couldn't bring themselves to finish that sentence.

All the town's children had their clay cuckoo pipes with them and they played a merry tune as they marched up Villa Villekulla's garden path. Tommy and Annika led the way. Just as they reached the veranda steps the door flew open and there stood Pippi in the doorway.

Her eyes were shining in her freckly face.

'Welcome to my humble abode,' she said,

and held out her arms.

Annika studied her carefully

so that she would be able to

remember

the way Pippi looked.

Never, ever, would she forget the way

she stood there with her red plaits

and her freckles and her beaming smile

and her big, black shoes.

In the background they could hear the muffled beating of a drum. Captain Longstocking was sitting in the kitchen with the drum between his knees. He was wearing his king's outfit again today. Pippi had asked him specially. She knew all the children wanted to see a real live Koratutt king.

The whole kitchen was filled with children who had gathered around King Ephraim and were staring at him. Annika thought it was lucky even more hadn't turned up, otherwise there wouldn't have been room. Just as she was thinking this she heard the sound of an accordion in the garden. And here came the entire crew of the *Hoppetossa*, with Fridolf leading the way! He was the one playing the accordion. Pippi had gone to the harbour that day to say hello to her friends and she had asked them to come along to the leaving party. She hurled herself at Fridolf and hugged him until he was blue in the face. Then she let him go and cried:

'Music! Music!'

So Fridolf played his accordion, King Ephraim banged his drum, and all the children played their clay pipes.

PIPPI HAS A LEAVING PARTY

The lid of the log box was closed and lined up on top of it were rows of lemonade bottles. On the kitchen table stood fifteen huge cream cakes and on the stove was a gigantic pot full of sausages.

King Ephraim started by grabbing eight sausages. Everyone followed his example and soon the only sound in the kitchen was the chomping of sausages. Then each and everyone could take as much cream cake and lemonade as they wanted. It was a bit squashed in the kitchen so the guests spilled out onto the veranda and into the garden, and everywhere cream cake shone white in the dusk.

When everyone was full up Tommy suggested they shake down the sausages and cake by playing a game. 'Simon Says', for example. Pippi didn't know how to play that game, but Tommy explained to her that one person was Simon and everyone else had to copy everything Simon did.

'Fine by me,' said Pippi. 'Sounds like a good game. But I'd better be Simon.'

She started by climbing onto the roof of the mangle shed. To do that you had to first balance on top of the garden fence, rest your stomach on the edge of the roof and then shuffle yourself up onto it. Tommy and Annika had done this lots of times so it was easy for them. But the other children thought it was quite difficult. Naturally, the sailors from the *Hoppetossa* were used to climbing up the rigging so for them it was a simple task, but Captain Longstocking found it harder because he was so fat. And he got his grass skirt caught. He panted heavily as he hauled himself up onto the roof.

'This grass skirt will never be the same again,' he said, gloomily.

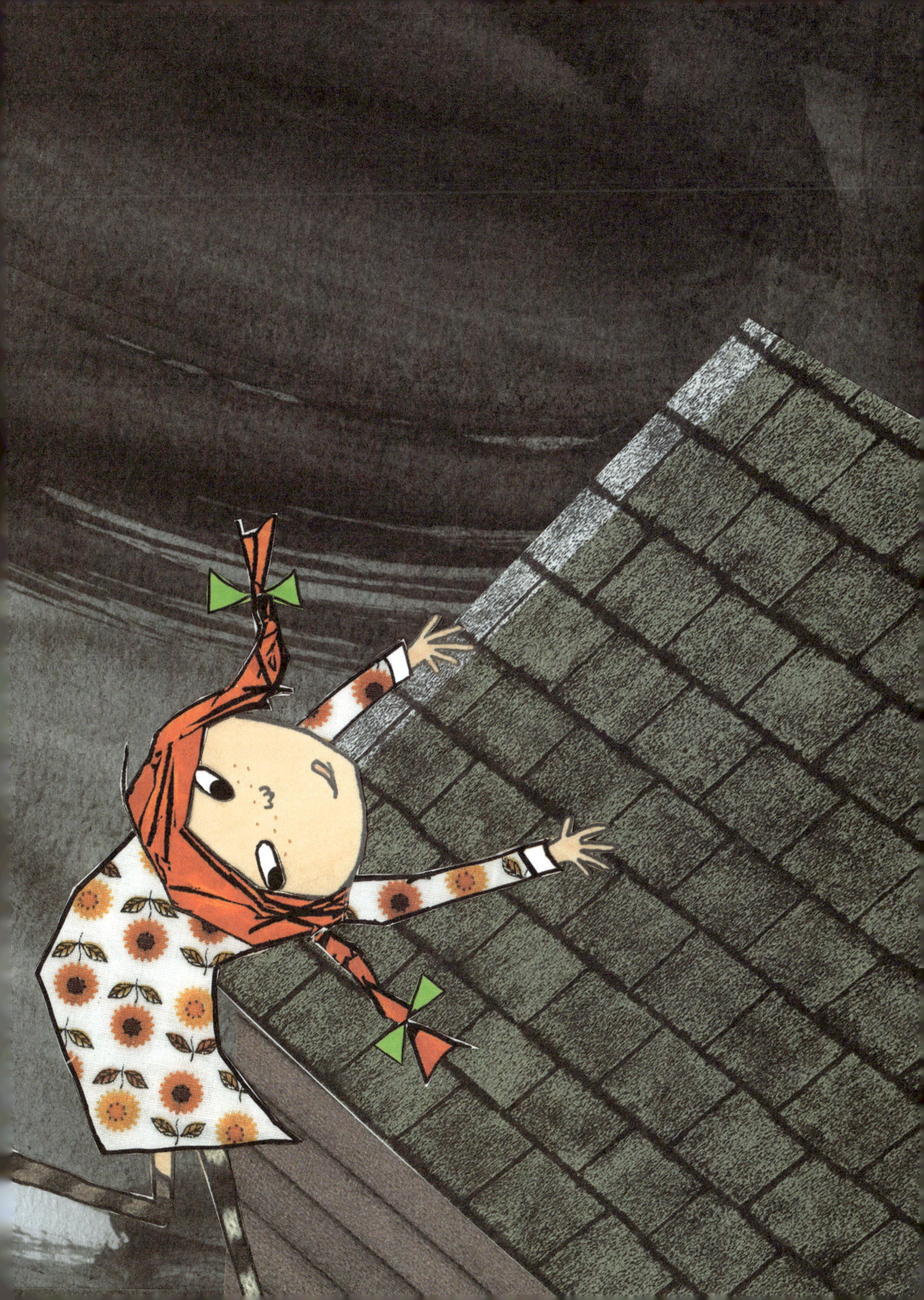

Then

Pippi

jumped

down

from

the

mangle

shed

roof

to

the

ground.

A number of the smaller children didn't dare, but Fridolf was very kind hearted and lifted them down. Next Pippi did six somersaults on the lawn. Everyone did the same, but Captain Longstocking said:

'Someone will have to give me a shove from behind or else I'll never manage.'

Pippi did it. And she made such a good job of it that once he started he couldn't stop, and he rolled like a ball over the grass and did fourteen somersaults instead of six.

Then Pippi dashed into Villa Villekulla,

ran up the stairs,

came

out

through

a window,

stood on the ledge and by stretching her leg

eally, really wide reached a ladder that was propped outside.

Without stopping she shot up the ladder, hopped onto Villa Villekulla's roof, ran along the top, jumped onto the chimney, stood on one leg and crowed like a cockerel. Then she threw herself headfirst into a tree that was growing at one end of the house, slid to the ground, rushed into the wood shed, picked up an axe and knocked out a plank in the wall, crept out through the narrow gap, jumped onto the wooden fence and balanced along it for at least fifty metres, climbed up an oak tree and then stopped for a rest among the branches at the very top.

Quite a crowd had gathered on the road outside Villa Villekulla, and afterwards they went home to say they had seen a king standing on one leg on Villa Villekulla's chimney calling out 'Cock-a-doodle-doo!' so loudly it could be heard for miles.

But no one believed it was true.

When Captain Longstocking tried to squeeze himself

through the narrow gap in the wall of the woodshed, the obvious thing happened—he got stuck and couldn't go either forwards or backwards. So the game was brought to an end and all the children clustered around to watch as Fridolf sawed Captain Longstocking out of the wall.

'That was a fair old game,' Captain Longstocking said, contentedly, when he had been set free. 'But what shall we think up now?'

'In the old days,' said Fridolf, 'The captain and Pippi used to compete to see who was strongest. That used to be mighty fun to watch.'

'Not a bad idea,' said Captain Longstocking. 'Trouble is, my daughter's getting stronger than I am.'

Tommy stood close to Pippi.

'Pippi,' he whispered. 'I was so afraid you were going to climb down into our hiding place in the hollow oak when we played Simon Says. I don't want anyone else to know about it. Even if we won't be going there ever again.'

'No, that's our secret,' said Pippi.

Her father had picked up an iron bar.

He bent it in the middle exactly as if it had been made of wax

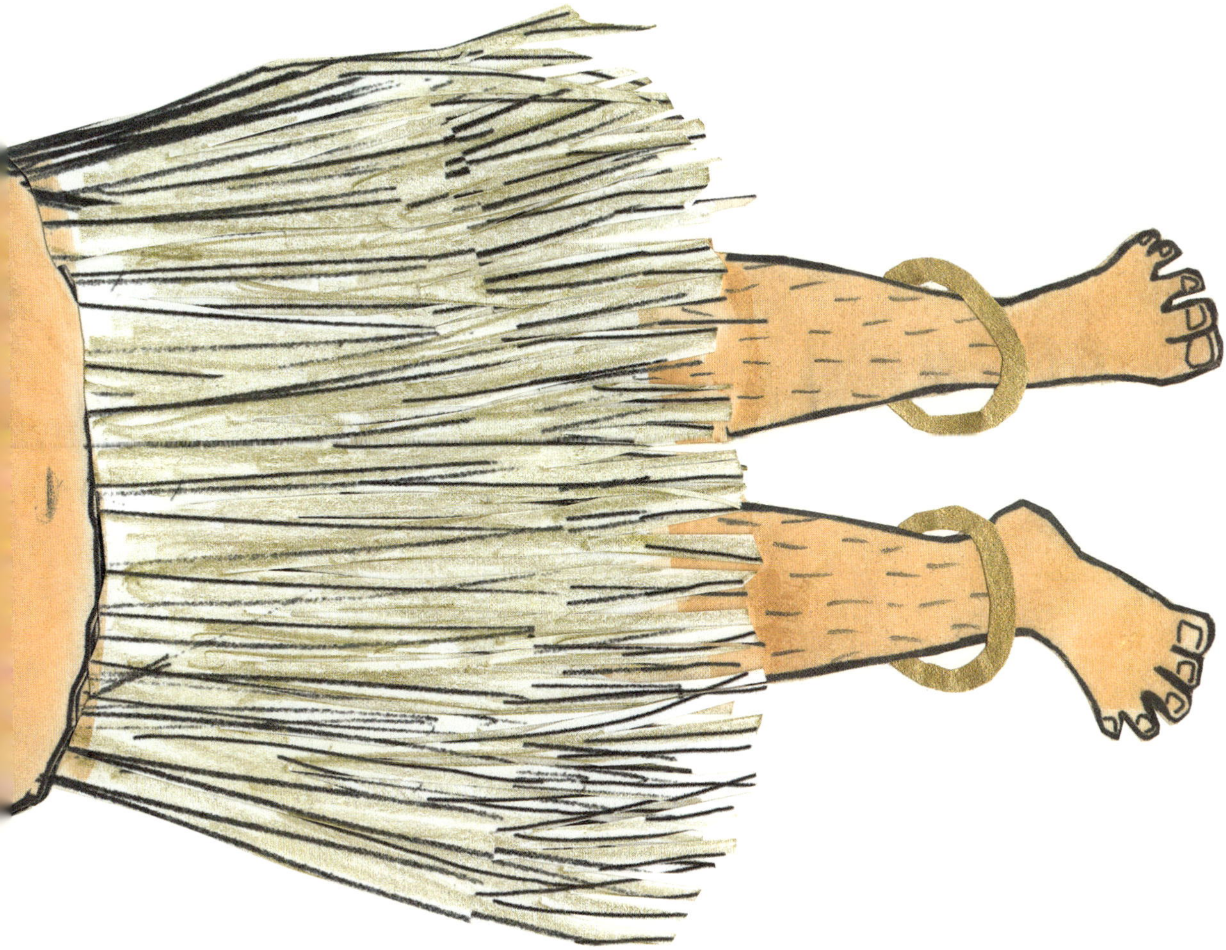

Pippi took another iron bar and did the same.

'Know what?' she said. 'I used to amuse myself with easy tricks like that when I was in my cradle. Just to pass the time.'

Then Captain Longstocking pulled off the kitchen door. Fridolf and seven other sailors were told to stand on the door and Captain Longstocking lifted them all high in the air and walked ten times round the lawn with them.

By now it was completely dark and Pippi lit torches here and there. They glowed so beautifully in the dark and threw magical shadows over the garden.

'Have you finished?' she called to her father after the tenth lap. He had. Then Pippi sat the horse on the kitchen door, and on the horse's back she sat Fridolf and three other sailors, and each sailor was holding two children. Fridolf held Tommy and Annika. Then Pippi lifted up the kitchen door and carried it round the garden twenty-five times, and it looked so graceful in the torchlight.

'Honest to goodness, child, you *are* stronger than me,' said Captain Longstocking.

PIPPI HAS A LEAVING PARTY

Afterwards they all sat together on the grass. Fridolf played his accordion and the other sailors sang the most beautiful sea shanties. The children danced to the music. Pippi held two of the flaming torches and danced more wildly than everybody else.

The party ended with a firework display. Pippi set off rockets and Catherine wheels so that the whole sky sparkled. Annika sat watching from the veranda. It was so beautiful, all of it. So lovely. She couldn't see the roses but she could smell their scent in the darkness. How wonderful everything would have been if only ... if only ... It felt like a cold hand was squeezing Annika's heart. And tomorrow—what would it be like then? And the rest of the summer holidays? And forever after? There would be no more Pippi in Villa Villekulla. No Mr Nilsson, no horse standing on the veranda. No more riding trips, no outings with Pippi, no nice evenings spent in Villa Villekulla's kitchen, no trees growing lemonade—well, the tree would still be here but Annika had a strong feeling that lemonade wouldn't be growing inside it after Pippi had gone. What would she and Tommy do tomorrow? Play croquet, presumably.

Annika sighed.

The party was over. All the children said thank you and goodbye. Captain Longstocking went with his crew back to the *Hoppetossa* and he thought Pippi should come as well. But Pippi said she wanted to spend one more night in Villa Villekulla.

'Tomorrow morning at ten sharp we raise anchor, don't forget!' called Captain Longstocking over his shoulder.

Now only Pippi, Tommy, and Annika were left. They sat on the veranda steps in the dark and were utterly silent.

'You can come here and play anyway,' said Pippi at last. 'The key will be on a nail beside the door. You can have everything in the bureau drawers. And if I put a ladder inside the old oak you can climb down yourselves. But you might not find quite so many bottles of lemonade growing there. It isn't the season.'

'No, Pippi,' said Tommy, solemnly. 'We won't be coming here any more.'

'No. Never, ever,' said Annika. And she thought that from now on she would shut her eyes every time

PIPPI HAS A LEAVING PARTY

she walked past Villa Villekulla. Villa Villekulla without Pippi—once again Annika felt that cold hand squeeze her heart.

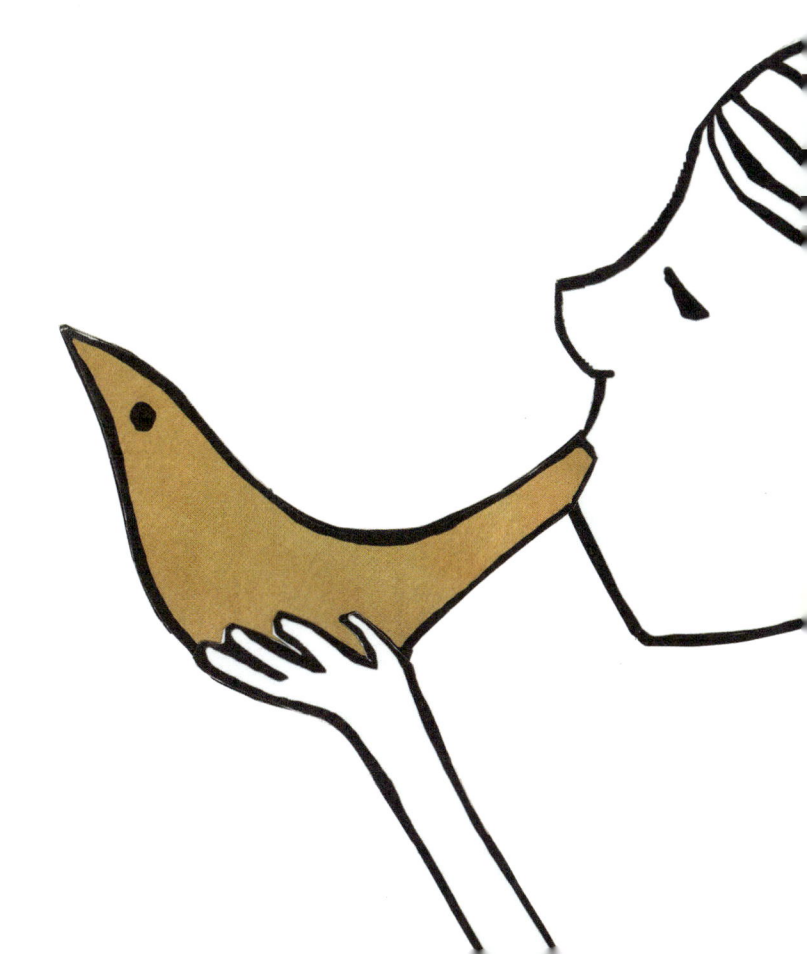

Chapter Nine: Pippi Goes Aboard

Pippi locked Villa Villekulla's front door securely and hung the key on a nail beside it. Then she the lifted the horse down from the veranda—for the very last time she lifted him from the veranda! Mr Nilsson was sitting on her shoulder already, looking important. He seemed to know that something special was happening.

'Well, that's about it,' said Pippi.

Tommy and Annika nodded. Yes, that was about it.

'It's still quite early,' said Pippi. 'Let's walk, it'll take longer.'

Tommy and Annika nodded again, but they said nothing. They started wandering towards town. Towards the harbour. Towards the *Hoppetossa*. The horse trotted along behind them.

Pippi looked back over her shoulder at Villa Villekulla.

'Nice place, that,' she said. 'No fleas, perfect in every way. And that's probably more than you can say of the mud hut I'll be living in from now on.'

Tommy and Annika said nothing.

'If my mud hut is swarming with fleas,' she went on, 'I'll tame them and keep them in a cigar box and play Last Pair Out with them every evening. I'll tie small bows around their legs and call the two most faithful and affectionate fleas Tommy and Annika, and they can sleep in my bed.'

Not even this could make Tommy and Annika speak.

'Blow me down, what's up with you two?' Pippi said, irritably. 'Let me tell you, it's dangerous to keep quiet for too long. Your tongue shrivels up if you don't use it. I knew a stove maker once in Kolkata who never spoke a single word. And look what happened to him. Once he was about to say to me: "Farewell Pippi, have a safe journey, it's been lovely," and can you guess what came out? First he pulled some awful faces because his mouth had rusted over, so they had to grease it with some sewing machine oil. And then he said: "**Foo booj oom mooj**!" I looked inside his mouth and guess what? His tongue looked like a wrinkled little leaf! For the rest of his life that stove maker could only say "**Foo booj oom mooj**!" It would be terrible if something like that happened to you two. Let's see if you can say it better than that stove maker: "Farewell Pippi, have a safe journey, it's been lovely." Go on, try!'

'Farewell Pippi, have a safe journey, it's been lovely,'

said Tommy and Annika obediently.

'Thank heavens for that,' said Pippi. 'Phew, you know how to give someone a scare! If you'd said "**Foo booj oom mooj**!" I don't know what I would have done!'

There was the harbour. There lay the *Hoppetossa*. Captain Longstocking stood on deck, shouting out the orders. The sailors sped here and there, getting everything ready for departure. All the people in the tiny little town had gathered on the quayside to wave Pippi off. And here she came, along with Tommy and Annika and the horse and Mr Nilsson.

'Here comes Pippi Longstocking! Make way for Pippi Longstocking!' they shouted, and people moved aside to let Pippi through. Pippi nodded and said hello to right and left. Then she picked up the horse and carried him up the gangplank. The poor creature stared around him suspiciously, because horses are not that keen on boats.

'So here you are, my beloved child,' said Captain Longstocking, stopping in the middle of giving an order to give Pippi a hug. He held her to his chest and they hugged each other so hard their ribs crunched.

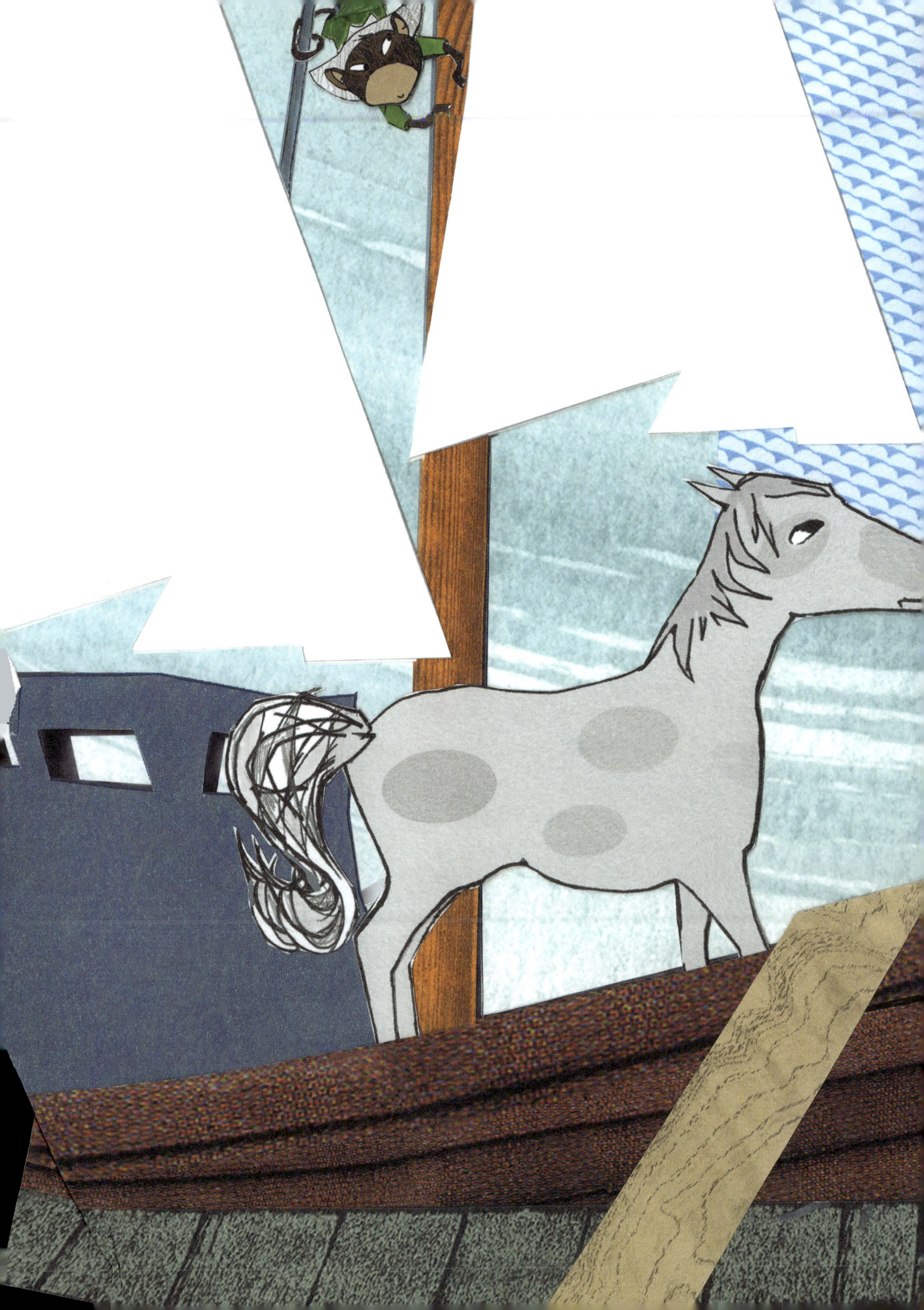

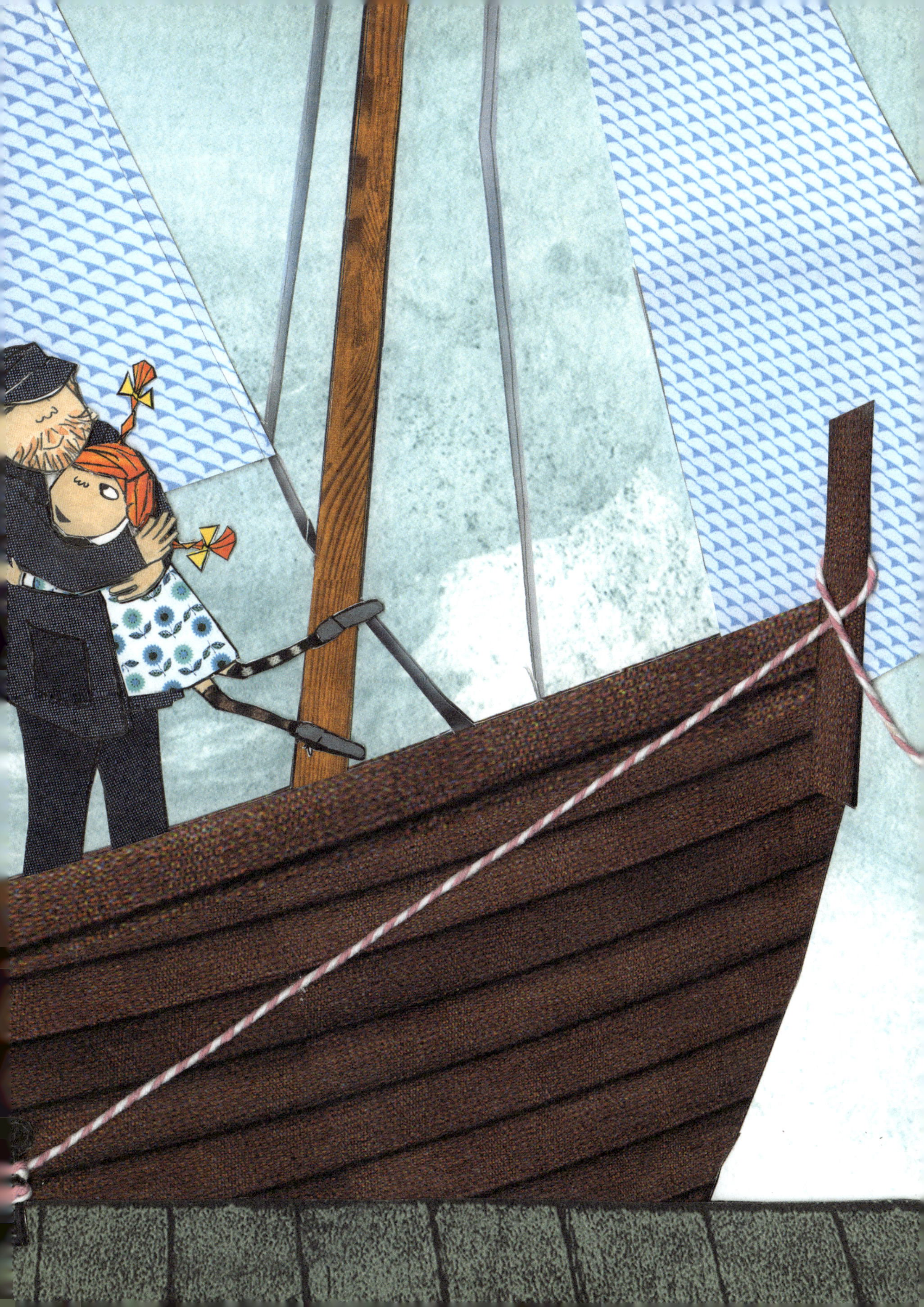

Annika had been walking around with a lump in her throat all morning, and when she saw Pippi carry the horse on board the lump dissolved into tears. She cried as she stood squashed against a crate on the quayside, quietly at first but gradually louder and louder.

'Stop wailing,' Tommy said angrily. 'You're showing us up in front of all these people!'

Being told off by Tommy only made Annika burst into floods of tears. She cried so hard she was shaking. Tommy kicked a stone and it rolled along the edge of the quay and plopped into the water. He would really rather have thrown it at the *Hoppetossa*, that horrible boat that was going to take Pippi away from them! Truth be told, if no one had been watching, Tommy would have howled as well. But that wouldn't do at all. He sent another stone flying.

Pippi came running down the gangplank. She rushed over to Tommy and Annika and took their hands in hers.

'Ten minutes to go,' she said.

That made Annika throw herself over the crate and cry as if her heart would break. There were no more stones left for Tommy to kick. He clenched his teeth and looked as if he could murder someone.

All the children of the tiny little town gathered around Pippi. They took out their clay cuckoo pipes and blew a farewell tune for her. It sounded indescribably sad because it was a very, very mournful little tune. Annika was crying so much by now that she could hardly stand. Just then Tommy remembered a goodbye poem he had written in Pippi's honour. He fished out a piece of paper and began to read. If only his voice wasn't trembling so much!

'Farewell and goodbye Pippi dear,
As you go away from here
remember friends will still be near,
year after year.'

'Oh, that's good. You made it rhyme all the way through,' Pippi said, pleased. 'I'll learn it by heart and read it to the Koratutts when we sit around the camp fire in the evening.'

Children pushed their way through from all directions to say goodbye. Pippi raised her hand, asking for silence.

'Children,' she said. 'From now on I will only have little Koratutts to play with. Who knows what we'll get up to? Perhaps we'll play tag with wild rhinoceroses and set up a snake charming business and ride elephants and swing between the palm trees round the corner. But we'll make the time pass somehow, I'm sure.'

Pippi paused. Tommy and Annika both felt they hated the children Pippi would be playing with in the future.

'But,' Pippi went on, 'perhaps a day will come during the rainy season, a boring day, because even though it's fun to run around naked in the rain you can't do more than get yourself wet. And when we've done that really properly perhaps we'll go into my mud hut—assuming the whole hut hasn't turned into a soggy mess, of course, in which case we'll make mud pies. But if it hasn't turned into a soggy mess we'll sit inside, the Koratutt children and me, and then perhaps the kids will say: "Pippi, tell us something!" And then I'll tell them about a tiny little town far away in another part of the world, and about the little children who live there. "You won't believe how sweet those children are," I'll say. "They blow on clay cuckoo pipes and—best of all—they can do multikipperation." But that might make the Koratutt children absolutely miserable because *they* can't do multikipperation, and then what will I do with them? Still, if the worst comes to the worst I'll pull my hut down and squish up the mud and we can bury ourselves in it up to our necks. It would be most unusual if I couldn't get their minds off multikipperation. Thanks, all of you. Goodbye, goodbye!'

The children blew their clay pipes and this tune was even sadder than the last one.

'Pippi, time to come aboard!' called Captain Longstocking.

'Aye, aye, Captain,' said Pippi.

She turned to Tommy and Annika and looked at them.

What a strange look, thought Tommy. It was exactly the same look Tommy's mum had on her face once when he was very, very ill. Annika was a small heap on the crate. Pippi lifted her up into her arms.

'Goodbye, Annika, goodbye,' she whispered. 'Don't cry!'

Annika threw her arms around Pippi's neck and gave a little whimper.

'Goodbye, Pippi,' she managed to say through the sobs.

Pippi took hold of Tommy's hand and squeezed it hard. Then she ran up the gangplank. That's when a large tear trickled down Tommy's nose. He gritted his teeth but that didn't help. Another tear fell. He took Annika's hand and they stood there, watching Pippi. They could see her on deck, but everything is always a bit blurred when you're looking through tears.

'Long live Pippi Longstocking!' shouted the people on the quayside.

'Raise the gangplank, Fridolf,' shouted Captain Longstocking.

And Fridolf did. The *Hoppetossa* was ready to sail away to foreign lands. But then . . .

'No, Daddy Ephraim,' Pippi said. 'This won't do. I can't bear it!'

'What can't you bear?' asked Captain Longstocking.

'I can't bear someone on God's green earth crying and being sad because of me. Lower the gangplank again! I'm staying in Villa Villekulla!'

Captain Longstocking was silent for a while.

'You do what you want,' he said finally. 'That's what you've always done!'

Pippi nodded.

'Yes, that's what I've always done,' she said, quietly.

And so they hugged each other, Pippi and her father, and made their ribs crunch again. And they agreed that Captain Longstocking would come to visit Pippi in Villa Villekulla very often.

'Anyhow, Daddy Ephraim,' said Pippi. 'It's probably best for a child to have a proper home and not roam the oceans so much or live in a mud hut, don't you think?'

'You're right as always, my daughter,' said Captain Longstocking. 'Without a doubt you'll have a more organized life in Villa Villekulla. And I expect that's best for little children.'

'Precisely,' said Pippi. 'It's absolutely best for little

children to have a
more organized life.
Especially if they can organize it themselves!'

Then Pippi said goodbye to the sailors on board the *Hoppetossa* and gave her father one last hug. She lifted up the horse in her strong arms and carried him down the gangplank. The *Hoppetossa* raised the anchor, but at the last second Captain Longstocking thought of something.

'Pippi!' he yelled. 'You must have some more golden coins! Catch this!'

And he threw her another bag full of golden coins. Unfortunately, the *Hoppetossa* had sailed too far away from the quayside and the bag missed the quay. 'Plop,' it said, and sank. A sigh of disappointment ran through the crowd. But then there was another 'plop'. It was Pippi, who had dived into the water. Up she came again with the bag between her teeth. She clambered onto the quay and pulled off some seaweed that was stuck behind her ear.

'Ha, now I'm as rich as a mountain troll again,' she said.

Tommy and Annika still hadn't worked out what had happened. They stood there gaping, staring at Pippi and the horse and Mr Nilsson and the bag of gold and the *Hoppetossa* that was steering under full sail out of the harbour.

'Aren't... aren't you on the boat?' spluttered Tommy at last.

'Give you three guesses,' said Pippi, wringing the water out of her plaits.

Then she lifted Tommy and Annika and the bag of gold and Mr Nilsson onto the horse and swung herself up after them.

'Back to Villa Villekulla!' she shouted, deafeningly.

Then, at last, Tommy and Annika understood. Tommy was so stupendously happy that he immediately burst into his favourite song, 'Here come the hurly-burly Swedes!'

Annika had been crying so much she couldn't stop straight away. She was still sniffing, but they were small, happy sniffs that would soon stop altogether. She felt Pippi's arms tight around her waist. It felt wonderfully secure. Oh, everything was wonderful!

PIPPI LONGSTOCKING GOES ABOARD

'What shall we do today, Pippi?' asked Annika, when she had finished sniffing.

'Um, play croquet, perhaps?' said Pippi.

'That would be nice,' said Annika. She knew even croquet would be different so long as Pippi was playing.

'Or . . .' said Pippi, and waited.

All the children of the little town crowded around the horse to hear what Pippi would say.

'Or . . .' she said. 'Or . . . we could go down to the river and practise walking on the water.'

'People can't walk on water,' said Tommy.

'Oh yes they can, it's not entirely impossible,' said Pippi. 'Once, in Cuba, I met a tailor who . . .'

The horse began to gallop and the children who had crowded around him couldn't hear how the story continued. But they stood for a long, long time, watching Pippi and her horse gallop in the direction of Villa Villekulla.

Soon they were only a tiny dot

far away.

And finally they vanished completely.

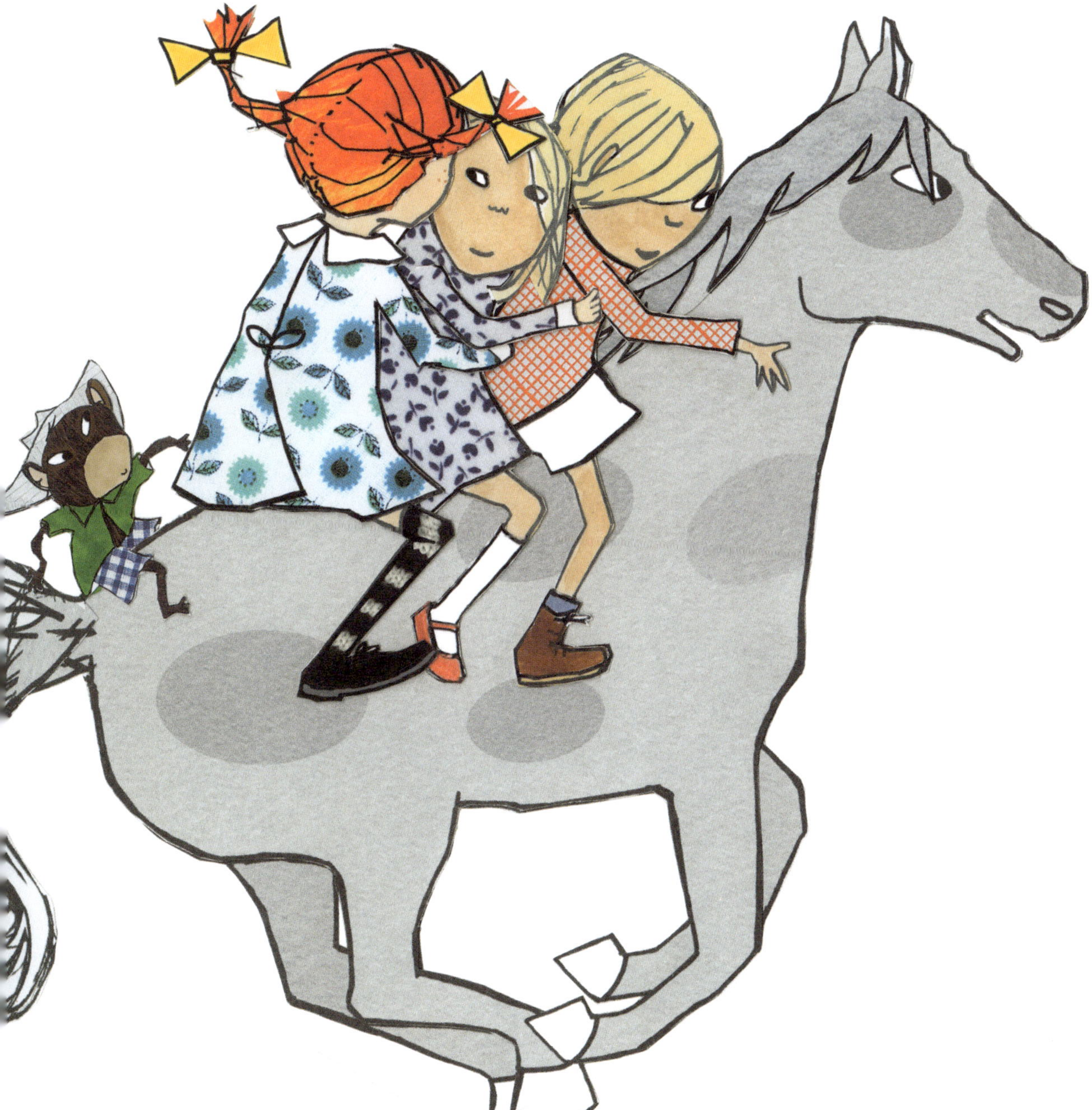

Astrid Lindgren was born in Sweden in 1907. She created stories about a free-spirited, red-haired girl to entertain her daughter, Karin, who was ill with pneumonia. The girl's name 'Pippi Longstocking' was in fact invented by Karin. *Pippi Longstocking* was published in 1945 and was an instant success. Astrid Lindgren once commented about her work, 'I write to amuse the child within me, and can only hope that other children may have some fun that way, too.' Astrid went on to write 75 books that together have sold 165 million copies and have been translated into more than 100 languages. She was awarded dozens of Swedish and international prizes, among them the prestigious Hans Christian Andersen medal in 1958. She died in 2002 and her memory is honoured by the Astrid Lindgren Memorial Award, founded in her name by the Swedish government and presented every year to authors, illustrators, storytellers, or advocates of reading for children and young people. For more information visit *www.astridlindgren.com*

Lauren Child has always loved Astrid Lindgren's books. She vividly remembers the first time she read *Pippi Longstocking:* 'I discovered Pippi Longstocking when I was about eight years old and found her completely inspiring. She caught my imagination, influenced my games, and has had a lasting impact on my work. I suppose the real key to Pippi is that she is an entirely free spirit: she is a girl who is both exciting and funny, refreshing to encounter even after all these years.' As the creator of some equally feisty little girls – notably Clarice Bean and Lola – Lauren has brought her own inimitable style to this beautifully illustrated edition of *Pippi Longstocking Goes Aboard*. Lauren Child is a multi-award-winning, bestselling writer and artist whose books are known and loved the world over. Between 2017 and 2019 she held the role of Waterstones Children's Laureate. For more information visit *www.milkmonitor.me*

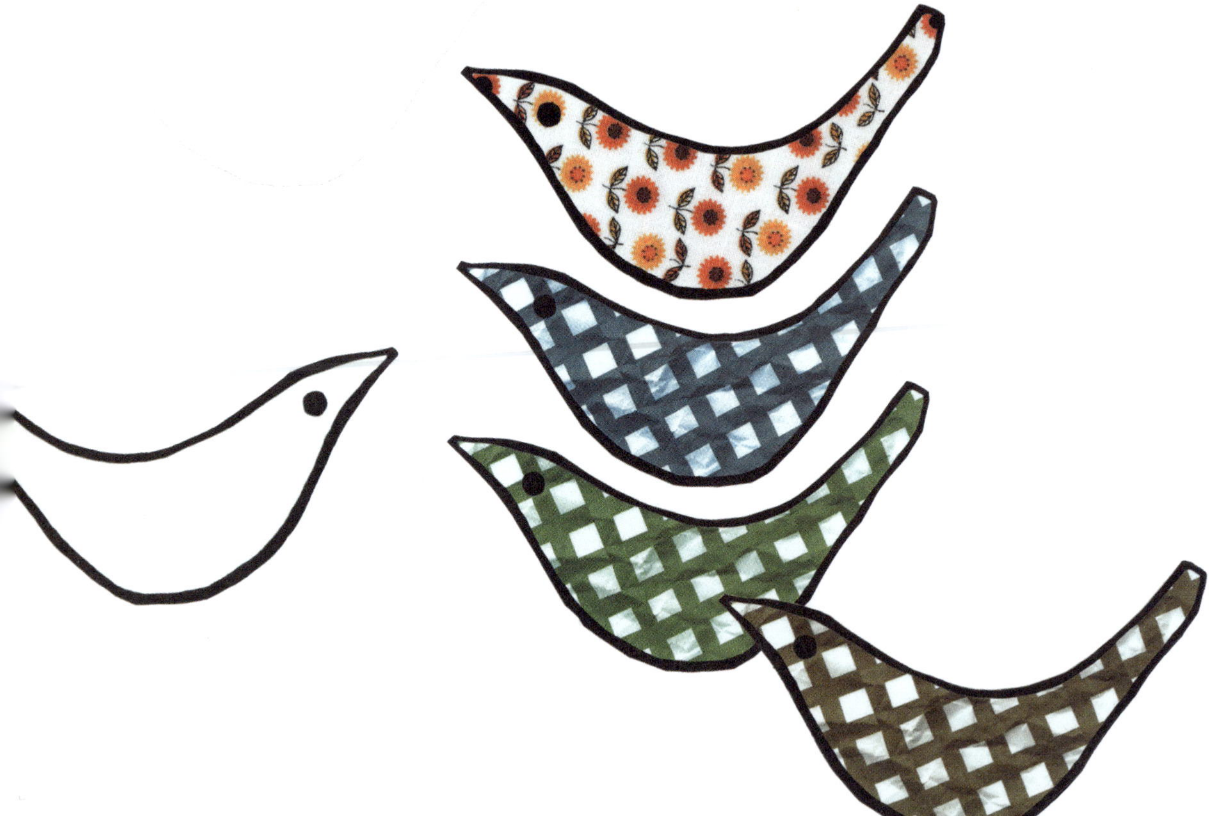